FAR FROM PHOENIX

FAR FROM PHOENIX
LAURENT SEKSIK

TRANSLATED FROM THE FRENCH
BY WILLARD WOOD

SALAMMBO
PRESS LIMITED

First published in the United Kingdom in 2017 by Salammbo Press
39A Belsize Avenue, London, NW3 4BN
www.salammbopress.com

Originally published in the French language as *La Légende des Fils*
© Flammarion, Paris, 2011

The moral right of Laurent Seksik to be identified as the author of this work has been
asserted in accordance with the Copyright, Designs and Patents Act 1988

This book is supported by the Institut français (Royaume-Uni)
as part of the Burgess programme
(www.frenchbooknews.com)

INSTITUT
FRANÇAIS
ROYAUME-UNI

A CIP catalogue record for this book is
available from the British Library

Cover design: John Oakey

ISBN 978-0-9932344-2-2

To my mother
To my father

I

Scott opened his eyes wide, flipped back the quilt, stopped the alarm clock, sat on the edge of the bed, looked around dazedly. A hint of light was coming into the room. He rubbed his eyes, examined the crucifix on the wall, took a deep breath. Lord, the hour is come, give me strength, watch over my mother while I am away, protect her from the devil who inhabits this place. He said amen and made the sign of the cross. He took off his pyjamas, pulled on his pants, his shirt, slipped into his Clarks, and stood. His glance fell on the photograph of President Kennedy tacked to the wall, one he'd clipped from the Sunday magazine. The president was extending his hand to a young boy. He imagined he was that boy.

He took from the dresser the letter he'd written the previous night, placed it on the quilt, took a step back, approved the effect.

He grabbed his canvas bag, which held a few clothes, a canteen, and a knife, passed into the dining room, stopped at the sideboard, opened the first drawer, snagged with his fingertips the roll of ten-dollar bills hidden in the back, slipped it into his pocket, returned everything to its place, and prayed the Lord to forgive him.

Halfway down the hallway, he caught sight of the Winchester hanging on the wall. He stood on tiptoe, took hold of the rifle, and carried it toward the room where his father slept. He cracked the door open, saw Jeffrey Hatford asleep, looking odd because his eyes were half-shut though he was in deep slumber.

He stood there motionless, holding the Winchester in his hand, looking at the man sprawled across the bed. How would it feel to aim a gun at the author of his days? He kept the muzzle pointed at the ground, turned, put the weapon back in its bracket, went out of the house, and closed the door quietly behind him. Shouldering his bundle, he strode down the path drawing the cold air of the plains deep into his lungs.

#

He was ready to cross valleys teeming with sequoias, vast deserts where stars slept. He would travel beside mountains that reared like islands into the sky, mesas of red sandstone with gigantic shadows. Ocotillo bushes would unfurl patterns of light at his feet. He would enter aspen forests steeped in silence, traverse canyons as deep as the ocean. Among amber-scented hills, big dark clouds pierced by shafts of light would throw rainstorms across his path and guide him toward the place of his dreams, the splendid spell-haunted world of the Gulf of California, where the horizon widens and the sea withdraws.

He looked at his watch. The hands pointed to six. At this moment, his mother would be ending her night shift. She would be getting ready to leave Memorial Hospital in Phoenix. Pulling on her beige wool coat directly over her nurse's uniform, she would be hurrying toward the Greyhound shuttle on Main Street, crossing in the middle of deserted blocks for fear of missing her bus and having to wait for the next one in a tide of glacial gray air.

A sermon by the Reverend Simpson came into his head. The pastor had spoken of irreparable offenses, citing as instances Joseph being sold into slavery by his brothers and Cain killing Abel. The meaning of the words suddenly leaped out at him. Lord, am I my mother's keeper?

The one commandment that his mother asked him to follow was not to lie. He had hidden the news that he was leaving. He had avoided her questions a few days ago, when she had almost penetrated his secret. He had denied it. He had betrayed her. He was leaving her a prey to inequity, to insults, to braggadocio. She would live the rest of her life convinced that she had given birth to a monster, a deserter, a hooligan. The son she loved was a delinquent, a coward.

He had the odd trait that he physically experienced what his mother was feeling. When the expression on Mom's face was happy, carefree, invulnerable, he would feel light and intensely joyful. When his mother was sad, the world around him lost all grace, all charm, all mystery.

Some nights, he was pulled from his sleep by noises in the hallway. It was Mom, with one of her terrible migraines, pacing through the house. Her shuffling feet tracked the course of her suffering. Lying in bed, Scott could picture her haggard face, the pain boring into her skull. He prayed to God, begged for it to stop. He accompanied Mom on her sleepless night, as he would have gone outside with her if she had wandered out into the night among the wild dogs. Suddenly, he heard nothing. The headache had been driven off. Mom had gone back into her room. The house was restored to calm. Scott lay there a long time with his eyes open before falling asleep. In the morning, both mother and son wore the same stigmata from the battle.

Scott contracted his mother's despair the way he caught the contagious illnesses that Mom brought back from the hospital. He loved it when his mother gave him the flu. He looked forward to flu season, waited impatiently for winter. The illness kept him in bed.

Mom would sit at his bedside. His father would go off. Scott would make his mother promise never to return to Memorial Hospital. His fever would rise. He would start to tremble. He was freezing, exhausted, broken. Mom spooned medicine into him, sponged his face, surrounded him with attention, whispered endearments, hummed little songs. Three days later, the fever had dropped. The telephone would ring. Doctor Jenkins's emergency room required the presence of Nurse Hatford. Your bad mother is going to have to leave. He used tricks to keep her from going, made himself vomit, coughed his lungs out. That night she would be gone. He was alone, cold. He should have been sad. The memory of the days just passed would drive his grief away—he would dwell on the words, the gestures, the looks. He consoled himself with bits of memory.

The next day, his father would come back. The air would become unbreathable. His mind would start making plans to run away.

Where had he found the strength to leave home? How had he ever plotted such a sacrilege? Abandon his mother! Was his father's madness contagious? The idea that he could share his father's traits frightened him. People say I have Mom's eyes and her smile. But what if I received my father's soul? What if the spirit of the Crooked One has entered into me? He'd lied, he'd stolen, he'd betrayed. He was in the act of becoming a Hatford!

He deliberately quickened his pace, walked a good distance along the road northward, forked off and climbed to the top of a butte overlooking the valley. The sun was rising behind the mountains. From his lookout, he could still see the house. He thought of the moment when his mother would come home. He imagined her gloomy and dispirited, laying her coat on a chair, dropping exhausted onto the couch. She would glance at the clock, go into the hallway toward his room, her face once again wearing the expression of tender joy that came over her at the thought of her son. She would carefully open his door. The empty room would lash out at her. She'd search every shadow, approach the bed, terrified, drawn by the letter on the covers. She'd read it. And here was the miracle he had hoped for: at the last sentence, her face would light up, cleansed of fear. It was the letter that brought about this wonder. Tears turned to laughter.

Awakened, his father would stand behind his mother's shoulder. Jeffrey Romuald Hatford would take the letter, read through it, tear it up, spit on it. The man would attack his wife, blame her for how she lived her life, order her to choose between her work and him, make threats against her son, heap insults on her, vow that there would be consequences, proper punishment. His eyes would be wild. His breath would reek of beer and cheap bourbon. He'd send plates flying. Mom would remain impassive. Her impervious calm would exacerbate his father's rage. In the end he would lift his hand to hit her. But at that moment—at least as Scott imagined it—the letter's warnings would come back to him. If you ever graze Mom's cheek with your hand... I'll be taller than you when

I come home. I'll tear you apart. I'll be a different man. I'll have learned to hit, to steal, to kill, who knows? You won't find me lowering my gaze anymore.

#

Looking out over the vast plain, he understood how great would be his mother's grief. He looked back along the way he had come, checked his watch. The 6:45 bus would soon drop Mom off at Route 17. He had a few minutes to get back to the house before she arrived and found his room empty. He abandoned his bag and started running.

He leapt. His feet kicked up dust. Each step gave him added speed, each stride was longer than the last. He felt no one could catch him. He was Willie Williams and Bob Hayes, he was the entire team of the Brooklyn Dodgers.

When he'd arrived back to within a few dozen yards of his house, he congratulated himself on being a sorcerer. He'd traveled back in time. He wiped away pain, he wiped away grief.

He opened the door quietly, crossed the living room, entered his bedroom. He tore up the letter, put the pieces in his pocket. He slid under the covers and waited, his eyes shut, for his mother to arrive.

II

A hand stroked his face. A kiss brushed his forehead, a voice whispered "Good morning" in his ear. He wanted to part his eyelids, throw his arms around Mom's neck, kiss her and hug her, properly celebrate her return. He held back. His father was sleeping in the next room. His snoring made the walls shake. One word, one sign of enthusiasm penetrating the partition between them and the man would come charging out, sputtering with rage.

Scott kept his eyelids shut. He preferred to safeguard the quiet of the moment, put off until later the show of happiness, the pleasure at being together again, the welcoming- home commotion. He'd wait until Jeffrey Hatford left home. He let his mother tiptoe away, draw the door closed behind her.

A moment later, his father's voice shouted through the house.

"You woke me up!"

"I'm sorry."

"And your being sorry is going to help me get back to sleep?"

"You'll wake Scott up."

"Oh, so your son's sleep is sacred, but mine doesn't matter! An invalid doesn't need sleep, is that it?"

Scott got out of bed, walked to the door as lightly as possible to keep the floorboards from squeaking.

"You make jokes about me and my bad leg, don't you, Doctor Jenkins and you? Or maybe the doctor just gropes you in silence?"

His father was talking like a thug. Propriety, compassion, respect were gone, and every sentiment by which men lived.

"Or maybe you're the one who pulls him down onto the bed? Then you start your moaning, I know that moaning of yours!"

Scott slipped into the hallway, saw his father a few yards from him, in the middle of the living room, back turned, powerful frame looming above his mother. He watched, a hidden spectator, wrapped in shadows, seemingly paralyzed, shrank against the wall, afraid of being noticed. I am a shadow on the wall, a creature of darkness, no one hears me, no one sees me.

"You find me disgusting, you go making whoopee with other men!"

His mother stood facing Scott, in front of his father, showing no trace of fear. She held her ground, undaunted, standing up to barbarism.

"You're not saying anything. Are you saving your voice for Doctor Jenkins?"

His father was behaving like an animal. You love nothing and no one, not even yourself, the one thing you worship is brute force, the one thing you obey is instinct. Force is your only language, violence your only recourse. You walk on ashes. You are ultimately accountable for your own unhappiness.

"You're surprised I know about your hanky-panky with Doctor Jenkins?"

Nothing will ever bring light to your vacant eyes. Your soul will feed on implacable   rages. You'll never know the sweetness of things.

"I could hit you…with this hand that has killed men!"

His mother didn't tremble, didn't lower her eyes. His mother was showing him how to act, teaching him bravery and faith, guiding him on the path of rebellion. He drew an intense energy from her behavior.

"Don't lift your hand against me!" she said.

Scott was about to interpose himself between them when he caught sight of the object hanging on the wall. Simultaneously, Jeffrey Hatford raised his fist, which was poised to come crashing down.

"Why aren't you looking at me?"

Scott's mother had noticed him, she looked at him as though mesmerized by the act he was about to commit. Scott had never seen her look at him that way. It made him feel enormously proud.

His father, sensing a presence at his back, turned around. The barrel of the Winchester pointed at him, startling him into a look of terror. But his fright was quickly replaced by a titanic rage.

"You're aiming a gun at your father?"

He nodded.

"You want to kill your father?"

He didn't answer.

"Go on, pull the trigger! Do you want me to show you how?"

Scott's hands started to tremble. He would have liked to explain his action to his mother, justify his violence. His mouth gaped soundlessly.

"Use your index finger, give it a squeeze, show me you're really a man! Prove to me you're a Hatford and not some fairy. Shoot! Go on, your father's telling you to!"

The weapon slid from Scott's hands and fell to the ground with a clatter. He lunged for the door, darted outside, crossed the rock garden, jumped the railing, raced up the path, arrived exhausted at the top of the hill.

#

His legs no longer supported him. His hands were still trembling. His heart was knocking against his rib cage. The town of Rolder below him looked like a chasm. The mountain ridges in the distance seemed to loom threateningly. The red earth towards the towns of Wayler and Dorth seemed to brim with lava. The wind, kicking up from the east, blew in misty clouds.

He sat on the edge of a rock, still panting with fear. He had experienced too many emotions, endured unmerited wrath. So many resolutions, so many moments of despair and elation had been packed into these hours. He couldn't ever remember a time in his life when misfortune had hit him so hard.

He peered at the house, tried to guess what was happening there, caught no sound of shouting or supplication. Could having a weapon pointed at him possibly have made his father listen to reason?

He hesitated to go back. He remembered a time when he had gone home immediately after an argument. He'd found the house steeped in silence. He'd slipped inside furtively, with the feeling that something was wrong. Holding his breath, treading with care, he'd advanced into the house with the confused sense that something dark and outside of his experience was happening. The door to the master bedroom was closed. From beyond it came muffled and indistinguishable sounds, of bodies rubbing, sighs being stifled, sheets rustling. He thought he heard his mother laugh. He left the house again disoriented, puzzled.

#

The air was charged with musk. Cascades of light spilled from every corner of the sky. The mist rose and fell on the hillsides. All was instilled with calm and indifference. His feverish mind slowly succumbed to the quiet majesty rising from the earth.

He hated his father. But the idea of killing him had never really entered his mind. Neither Jeffrey Hatford's face nor his corpse entered his dreams. Or only in a form he didn't recognize, a dream he no longer recalled. He remembered only his most beautiful dreams.

He told himself that his father would forget sooner or later. He believed in miracles, he always had. His faith had saved him, a golden light in the black wind. The Lord was just, He granted prayers, He resuscitated the dead.

He thought of his mother. When he saw her again, Mom wouldn't dwell on what had happened. She'd make only a passing reference to it. She'd quickly move on to a lighter and more cheerful topic. His mother was endlessly forgiving—goodness itself.

He looked out over the vast expanses submerged in light. High white clouds wove fine veils over the valley. The mountain chains rising in the distance formed a shelter from the wrath of men. The nearest houses gave off the sounds of happy voices. A hot wind blew through the valley. Everything seemed a long way off, softly murmuring and mantled in peace.

Soon Scott lost any sense of hostility or violence.

He spent the morning on top of the butte, idling near the ruins of a wooden structure that the older residents claimed to be the first building in town but that now sheltered only a few rats. In the afternoon he returned to town, went to the movies. He chose to see *West Side Story*, a movie that everyone was saying good things about. He hated the plot, laughed at the sight of New York City street gangs facing off by singing in falsetto and dancing like ballerinas.

As it was still too early to go home, he decided to see *Rio Bravo* again. He watched John T. Chance, the hero played by John Wayne, arrest a man called Joe Burdette for murder, saw Pat Wheeler gunned down from behind for having offered to help Chance, and witnessed Dude, played by Dean Martin, avenge Wheeler by shooting the man who'd murdered him. After which Chance meets Feathers, a dangerous beauty, played by Angie Dickinson. In the end, Chance, old Stumpy, and Dude rid the world of the lowlife Burdette brothers thanks to their trusty pistols and a few sticks of dynamite. Justice triumphs, and the guilty are punished.

When he got home, his mother had gone to work. His father was away, probably trying to drown his anger in the neighborhood bars.

III

Every weekday morning at about 7 o'clock, mother and son had a rendezvous on the side of Route 17 in front of the Rolder bus stop in the valley flats, a few miles from the entrance to town. The Greyhound bus that shuttled between Phoenix and Flagstaff would drop Mom off after her night shift at the hospital. Twenty minutes later, her son would climb aboard the bus going the other way, getting off near the Indian School in Phoenix. That twenty-minute gap was the time they had together. And since Mom left for work on weekdays before Scott returned home, they had no other place—except on Sundays—to see each other, no other time to talk.

Such was their life, made of moments snatched from the slow stream of the passing days, lonely expanses brightened by magic interludes. Every day, they went through the same ceremonial. In that brief space, they knew the joy of reunion and the grief of separation. Then twenty-four hours would elapse. Their shared moment gave rhythm to the weeks and months, gave a reference point to their existence. On some dreary afternoons, Scott would think: night will come, then it will be day and I'll see my mother.

Their time together was unstructured. There was never a set topic to discuss, never a question to avoid. The meetings often passed in a kind of elation, though sometimes the moment inclined toward sadness. It was all right to cry, and laughing was allowed. Some mornings they never stopped talking, others they kept quiet. The time seemed just as long whether they said something crucial or were quiet. They rarely spoke about the past, they never looked toward the future. They celebrated the present moment.

Neither had ever mentioned this daily meeting to anyone else, and most likely no one had ever noticed the little game these two played, early in the morning, in this nowhere valley, along a deserted road. They felt protected there, surrounded by mountains. Their visiting room had the dimensions of the boundless day.

#

That morning Scott woke up even before the alarm clock went off. He had slept poorly. All night he had stewed over his bitterness, anger, and uncertainty. What if my index finger had tightened on the trigger? The hours slipped by like minutes. His eyelids refused to shut. Visions unspooled before him—a funeral procession wound its way through town, a man in a top hat was driving a '57 red Plymouth, a woman dressed in black read the lines of his hand, then looked at him with great sadness. He'd finally dropped asleep briefly.

He shrugged off the night, hauled himself out of bed, stumbled into the bathroom, splashed water on his face, combed his dark mane, tried to subdue the cowlick over his forehead, dressed, went into the kitchen, cooked two eggs for himself on the old electric stovetop, ate, drank his grapefruit juice, grabbed his book bag, and went out.

Looking toward the rising sun, with the town spread out below him, he thought of the great challenge that faced him daily: reaching Route 17 before the bus did, extending his hand to his mother as she came down the steps. He dreamed of standing there, tall and still, a soldier at attention, a princely escort, holding his breath, heart racing, chest swelled. His mother, suspended in air, would hold out her hand to him, as if they were to waltz. But up till now, he had always arrived too late. He never led the dance.

He launched himself down the track toward Rolder, a dirt road with wild grass on either side that descended in loops, a road the mayor had promised to give a name to but that, three years after the subdivision was finished, was still known only as "Blank Street." Scott wondered whether someone who lives in a nameless place deserves respect, whether the Hatfords might count for less than people from the lower town, less than the Delseys on Capitol Street, or the Matthews on Adview Road.

He passed the place known as "Los Lobos," where several Mexican families lived under one roof, reportedly a source of shady dealings, contraband cigarettes, and girls on the game around the Phoenix drive-ins. The kids, who were always on the street, sometimes ventured higher up the hill. Jeffrey Hatford would order them off, throw stones to make them clear out. They dodged the rocks, laughing hysterically, and taunted him with a name that made his anger boil over: "Yo, come here and say that, Gimpy Leg!" In the end, the man would have to go back inside, dragging his bad leg, while insults rained down on him.

Scott passed a house where two young Mexicans were holding a conversation on the stoop. The boys glared at him challengingly, then one of them flicked his lighted cigarette right at him. A bit of ash grazed his cheek.

At the bottom of Blank Street, he angled toward Seneca Square, an abandoned lot once planted with hazelnut trees but now overrun with brambles. He jumped through the bushes, leapt over puddles stagnating in runnels carved by the autumn rains. He pushed ahead into the empty streets of the town, just as the sky's growing pallor started to dispel the shadows. At the corner of Capitol Street, he lengthened his stride. Now he was in a race against the sun. If he wanted to arrive ahead of his mother, he had to reach Lincoln

Avenue before the sun cleared the top of the hill. It was still possible.

At 67 Oxford Street, he checked the windows on the second floor. A month earlier, he had seen a woman there, bare-breasted, looking out the window. Nothing, not even his cousin Mike's erotic magazines, had ever excited him as that vision had. Since then, an irresistible force stopped him when he reached the building. Today the curtains were drawn.

On Roosevelt, he found his old ally, Mr. Brown, his head under the hood of his ancient Model 52 Buick. Mr. Brown looked around as he passed and called out, "You'll get there, Scott! And if you don't, just let me know and I'll drive you…if I can ever get this dagnabbed car to start…" Scott remembered his mother's explanation of why Mr. Brown was so nice, "You remind him of the son he lost in Korea." The horrors of war could make men better? From watching his father, Scott had his doubts.

He passed a row of back yards, skirted a series of small, abandoned warehouses dating from a time when Rolder manufactured pots and pans, the town's glory days—if there was any pride in manufacturing pots and pans.

He crossed into Rolder's working-class neighborhood, through a maze of streets where the houses grew scarcer, their dirty gray facades crumbling with neglect. Here, families seemed intent on hiding their poverty behind bare fences and piles of bricks, while on the west side of town the people along Adview Road made a great show of their wealth. On Adview Road, teenagers cruised in late-model Chevrolets and Fords, to the envy of passersby, who were surprised to find so much wealth in Rolder when pots and pans hadn't been manufactured there for eons. He left the last house in town behind.

Now his race took him along Route 17. He ran down the highway, which was scattered with gravel and hedged in on either side by walls of honeysuckle. He passed a billboard bearing the gigantic head of a cow, intended as a promotion for dairy products. In his memory, it had always been there. The cow had seen him grow up, and it now watched him run past with the glum and indifferent stare that Scott considered Rolder's emblem.

The ground by the roadside was turning dry and desolate. He felt a stitch in his side, and his calves were cramping. The sun was distinctly above the hills. Cars moving at breakneck speed rushed past him, leaving clouds of sand in their wake. "You'll wind up smeared on Route 17 like a coyote," his father had predicted. He was getting close. He couldn't let himself be distracted. Forget the cars blaring their horns, don't bite the dust.

Partway up the hillside, on the enormous ranch belonging to the Eaches, he saw Ted, the youngest, riding a horse at full gallop. The boy seemed to fly over the plain.

Suddenly, as though materializing from his anticipation, the Greyhound bus appeared at the far point of the road, its headlights aimed at him. He forgot his exhaustion and the ache in his calves, gathered his strength and quickened his pace. Sweat dripped from him as he ran, flooding his eyes, blurring his vision. He'd lost all sense of distance. Nothing around him was still calm or peaceful. His slightly manic fever seemed to affect the earth and the sky, and in the trembling reflection of the mountain crests and ember-colored earth around him everything appeared fervently animated. The metal mass was approaching. The company's letters, painted in red on the front of the bus against a white background, sparkled in the white glare, grew before his eyes, portents of his loss in the race against time, broadcasting to the desert that he would again arrive too late. The growl of the engine grew louder every second, sounding the knell to his hopes, exposing the vanity of his battle. The crunch of the bus's tires told him he had lost the match. A cloud of dust formed in the middle of the road. The bus stopped a few yards ahead of him. The front door opened and a light-splashed figure emerged. His mother stepped onto the gravel.

He never arrived on time. Something in the air resisted his passage. Had his father put a curse on him? He would have liked to slice down the road, leap faster than the speed of light. No matter at what time he left, machine triumphed over man. He saw his mother's form emerge from the cloud of smoke. Every day ended in defeat. But he stayed confident. One day, he would be the winner in the race with time.

Mom held out her arms, her long, somewhat thin arms, in whose embrace he ran to nestle, to rest after his race, to extinguish the great fire that burned in his head as the sun cast its long shadows. She took a step back, looked searchingly at him as though the shape of his face or the color of his eyes could have changed in twenty-four hours. She wiped his forehead, smoothed his hair, straightened his shirt, pulled a water bottle from her handbag. He drank it to the last drop, then broke the silence.

"Are you angry with me about yesterday?"

"Angry at you? I only want you to forget what happened."

"I threatened my father with a rifle!"

"Don't think about it."

He promised to try. She combed her fingers through his hair, kissed him on the forehead.

"You're the nicest, handsomest boy your age. Handsomer than James Dean."

He took a letter from his pocket, handed it to his mother. It was the reply he'd written to Mrs. Lloyd, the municipal employee who'd acknowledged his request that Blank Street be given a proper name. He had devoted some time to composing the letter. He wanted her advice before mailing it. She read it out loud:

Dear Mrs. Lloyd, You can well imagine the delight with which I read your sympathetic letter. You have restored my faith in our county administration and raised it to a par with my faith in the Almighty. You are a true apostle of our mayor. You shepherd this town's business the way Peter shepherded the faithful toward Lake Tiberias. And just as Peter baptized, so you will give a real name to "Blank Street." You will abolish the division between us and the people of the lower town, the residents of Lincoln Street or Adview Road. You will give the Hatfords back their dignity—because not to have a real address is not to exist fully. Thanks again, dear Mrs. Lloyd, and God bless you, your family, and the office workers over whom you preside.

His mother said, "Do you want to know what I think? You're not only as handsome as James Dean, you're as intelligent as Bobby Kennedy!"

"Don't...don't say anything to my Dad. He'd be furious if he ever learned I was begging for help from the county authorities."

"Do I tell your father anything?"

"But I'd like him to know that I'm behind it if anything comes of my request. I'd like him...to be proud of me."

"I'm sure that he is. He's proud of you in his own way."

Using force was all his father knew. His father's only feelings for him were hatred and contempt. His father… She interrupted him to ask if his cousin Mike was going to wait for him later at the Phoenix bus stop. He knew that she didn't like Mike and found fault with him. Mike smoked, Mike drank. Mike flew into a rage over nothing. Mike was a liar. Mike claimed he knew where a treasure was hidden in Arizona. Mike insisted he had traveled by plane. Mike had supposedly seen the Chicago Cubs give the Mets a drubbing. Mike said that he spoke to his father at night in his room and that he could hear his father answered him—Richard Alan Hatford had died in the Korean War.

"Mike is a thief too, isn't he?" said his mother.

Mike owned the most amazing collection of 45 rpm's, all of them shoplifted from Spiney's. And Mike sometimes tried to drag Scott along to Phoenix's drive-ins looking for girls. But he liked Mike anyway. Mike treated him as a brother.

"A liar, a self-aggrandizer, a bully, a thief… Mike's a real Hatford! Run, there's your bus, give me a kiss and go find your cousin."

He kissed her, hurried to the back of the bus, pressed his face against the rear window, and watched his mother grow small in the distance until she disappeared on the horizon. He stayed that way a few more seconds, waving into the void. When he turned around, he noticed several people looking at him and heard derisive laughter but ignored it.

IV

The road to Phoenix crossed a wild stretch of land rimmed by mountains. In the distance the horizon curved, forming an arch. The early light raked over the rock, set fire to the sandstone cliffs. No shadow, anywhere, met the beholder's eye, except where a row of saguaros lifted their spine-covered arms heavenward as though praying to God. Was there as majestic a world anywhere else, without beginning or end?

The man next to Scott was leafing through a newspaper. The boy read over his shoulder. On every page, the headlines spoke of war. Krushchev was threatening America. The Soviets had built missile silos on Cuba. The biggest cities in the U.S.A. lay within their range. An attack was imminent. Five hundred thousand Marines had been placed on a war footing. The U.S. Navy's ships patrolled the Caribbean Sea. Bombers and U-2's had been seen flying over Phoenix. The Third World War would break out any day.

"You interested in this, sonny?" said the man.

Scott shook his head. He didn't want to hear about war. His father had taken part in two armed conflicts, in Europe and South Korea. His father had left part of his thigh on the battlefield and probably most of his soul.

"War is what's made America what it is—that and the dollar, the family, and private property. Every generation has its war. You'll go to war some day too."

Scott nodded, opened his bookbag, pulled out a book and started to read. The man didn't insist.

The book was one that his cousin had lent him. It was called *Stories of the Sioux,* written in 1934 by a certain Luther Standing Bear, and Scott found it fascinating. His cousin's tastes were always on target. Mom was too hard on Mike. Life hadn't exactly showered him with favors. Mike had lost his father in Korea when he was seven. He hadn't known his mother. He now lived with his aunt, his mother's sister. Everyone might consider Mike a somewhat unreliable teller of tall tales, but his friendship was worth a lot. Mike was fearless, generous, and loyal—he came to Scott's defense when the kids at school picked on him. And no one told a story better than Mike. For Scott, who had never been outside of Rolder, Mike's store of adventures seemed inexhaustible. He would recount a World Series game, and you were watching it from the stands. He described the war, and you were a Marine living through hell. He talked about the girls in high school, and they were standing naked in front of you. What did it matter that he had never really been aboard a Delta Airlines Boeing 727, or attended the Chicago Cubs' rout of the Mets, or that his father didn't really answer when Mike spoke to him in the silence of his room?

Mike was nothing like the degenerate scamp he took pleasure in pretending to be—this boy who could use his fists like a pair of sledgehammers and gobble down two hamburgers in a row at Walt's. You only had to see him cry like a baby over the last scene of *The Misfits,* as Scott had a few months ago .

#

Mike had shared his interest in horses and cowboy films, the ones that didn't portray Indians as savages. In just a year, Mike had taken him to see: *The Tall Men, The Last Sunset, The Big Trail, The Horse Soldiers, Rio Grande, Two Rode Together, Three Godfathers, The Searchers, The Big Land*—twice—and *Broken Arrow,* the first movie to restore dignity to the Indian people, and which Mike and he had seen countless times. Recently, he'd loved Marlon Brando in *One-Eyed Jacks.* Mike had also gone with him to see *The Roots of Heaven,* which was not about Indians or horses but about elephants, and it had proved as deeply moving as *The Big Land.*

#

A few months ago, Mike told him the most amazing story he'd ever heard. Mike had heard the story from his father, and Richard Hatford had told it to him a few weeks before leaving for Korea.

In the Gulf of California, some fifty miles east of the mouth of the Colorado River, near a small lake, the East River takes its source. It winds through narrow gorges with pine trees clinging to the rock. Almost at the gulf, the river emerges from the canyons and flows quietly beside sandstone hills. It flows lazily through an expanse of reeds, only to spill into the sea at a tawny sandbank, ringed by the inlets of a mountain whose cliffs drop sheer into the Gulf of California. The place does not appear on any map. Once a year, on this stretch of sand unknown to man, there happens something that Mike's father claimed to have been the only human ever to see.

On the day of the summer solstice, shortly after daybreak, the beach starts to echo with a dull rumbling. A whirlwind of dust forms in the uplands, floats down from the hills, twirls above the river's waters. The rumbling grows to a din. Suddenly, the shapeless mass of some fifteen mustangs barrels toward the beach. The horde reaches the strand. The horses advance, lined up like companions in arms. Their hooves drum dully over the sand. Their neighing vibrates on the breath of the wind. The beasts file past, disdainful, their eyes sparkling in the bright light, their coats reflecting the sky's hues. So orderly is the cavalcade, so coordinated the battalion, it seems that one of the animals must be setting the pace. They are proud wild horses, but from their lumbering grace, their labored gait, it's clear that they're all advanced in age. The animals pursue their course unperturbed. Their hooves sink into the sand. Now they trot into the waves. They continue forward, the water reaching their knees. The mass of their bodies sinks slowly. Nothing stops the animals, and nothing frightens them. The herd pushes ahead into the line of breakers, a flood of foam in its wake. The horses charge toward destruction. Soon, only their necks are above water. Their tails float behind them. Not one of the horses balks, not one turns back. Is it determination or are they unaware of the danger? Their bodies sink below the water's surface. Only their heads emerge. Not one turns around, not one renounces its grisly fate. The cavalcade is entirely submerged in the deep waters. Nothing is left of the splendid animals. The sea foam closes over their bodies. The mustangs have disappeared in the midst of this Eden. Now the waves disperse the last traces of the beasts. No corpse floats to the surface or washes up on shore. The water has swallowed everything up. The sea keeps its bodies in its darkest depths. The sea is a tomb.

Scott was convinced that the mustang graveyard was not a legend. Mike would never have invented such a story. The tale was his only legacy from his father. Mike might steal, smoke, and drink, but he would never invoke the shade of Richard Hatford to prop up a lie. The Hatfords might do violence to the living, but they respected the memory of the dead.

V

Scott stepped off the bus at Washington Street. Before his foot touched the asphalt, a sauna's humid heat enveloped him. Not a wisp of breeze. The heat stopped time in its tracks.

Mike stood a short way down the sidewalk, a cigarette in his mouth. The two cousins exchanged greetings and started toward the bus stop where they would catch the No. 43 to school. Men in business suits hurried past, their faces serious. Women with their hair in identical, carefully formed chignons and wearing skirt suits, usually gray, clicked their heels on the pavement, entered office buildings, raised an arm to flag down a taxi.

"Mike, do you think there'll be a war?" asked Scott.

"The Commies can supposedly wipe out our cities. But why would anyone target Phoenix? You'd have to be really depraved. I know a guy, a former Marine, who's invented an antinuclear protective suit. That'll save us."

"Could you get one for my mother?"

"I'll pass on the order. And I'll buy one for Alison. Have I told you about Alison?"

He had talked about Alison a lot, her blue eyes, her voluptuous breasts, her endless legs, the strange and novel sensation he'd felt when he inserted a finger between her thighs.

"I'd rather hear you talk about mustangs."

"You're weird. You like horses better than girls!"

After thinking for a moment, Mike launched into the story of the Navajos when they made their stronghold along the East River and scattered their ancestors' ashes in its waters. The place was cursed. White Belly, a cousin of Sitting Bull, had been thrown off a cliff with all his men by Custer's soldiers. The women of the clan, including Long Braid, White Belly's squaw, had been raped and bludgeoned to death with stones before they were all thrown off the cliff too.

"You believe me, don't you?"

"Of course I do, Mike!"

"Some people don't believe me. Just because my father's dead, they think I make things up. But not having a father doesn't keep you from telling the truth, does it?

"Just the opposite."

Mike stopped in the middle of the sidewalk, put his bookbag down, pulled out a package wrapped in newspaper, and handed it to his cousin.

"A present!" he said.

Scott unwrapped the package with slightly trembling hands. There were four books inside: *The Naked and the Dead,* by Norman Mailer, *Geronimo's Story of his Life,* by S. M. Barrett, *Franny and Zooey,* by J. D. Salinger, and a collection of poems by Robert Frost. It was the first time Scott had ever received a present from anyone but his mother. He choked up.

"Don't blubber, Scott. Those books didn't cost me a cent."

"You mean you stole them?"

"You don't think I have enough money to go out and buy four new books, do you?"

"But…you aren't supposed to steal books!"

"Why not? I steal 45 rpm's and cigarettes."

"There are laws about it in…in the Constitution."

"Are you kidding? The Constitution gives me the right to buy a machine gun. Why is it wrong to steal something that's meant for everyone? Shouldn't we be allowed to read these books too? What are we guilty of? Stealing? You're wrong there, cousin. We're only guilty of being poor."

Scott pushed the books away a second time.

"What? I give you a present, and you then call me a thief? You disparage my family, my father's memory! Are you jealous because my father died a hero in Korea? Not like yours, who shot himself in the foot."

"Who caught a bullet in the upper leg."

"Oh, when we're talking about mustangs, you're willing to be my friend. But as soon as it gets personal, you look down your nose at me! You put on that superior air."

"I promise I don't have a superior air."

"You can't even see it. You're not doing it on purpose. That's even worse. You do it in spite of yourself."

"I'm sorry, Mike, I promise I'll keep the books. Thanks, thanks with all my heart."

"OK, I like that better! For a moment, I didn't think you had a heart."

They walked together along Van Buren Street, while an uneasy silence settled between them. After a while, Mike spoke again:

"I apologize for saying your father dodged combat... It isn't true, and my father had a lot of respect for yours."

"It's good to hear that someone held my father in respect."

"My father really wanted to follow his example and take part in a landing under enemy fire. People only talk about D-Day, but MacArthur's landing in Inchon Bay was something too, wasn't it?"

"Red Beach was every bit as amazing as Omaha Beach."

"Yeah, maybe for you. But everyone else has already forgotten the Korean War. Fifty thousand American soldiers were killed, not exactly nothing! Land of the Morning Calm, yeah, right! A million Chinese were shooting at our boys like rabbits! My father died outside Seoul. If he'd lived another few days, Seoul would've been in American hands."

"It was fate, Mike. There wasn't anything he could do about it."

"With your father, it wasn't fate. And I'm sorry I implied he was a coward."

"You didn't mean any harm."

"It's great that my father went to join his brother. Nothing forced him to."

"It shows such family spirit."

"Yeah, too bad that war doesn't reward family spirit."

#

That afternoon after classes, Scott decided to return the books to the shop where they'd been taken. It wrenched his heart to give up the collection by Robert Frost, an author who exalted the simple glories of America like no one else. A year and a half earlier, at the president's inauguration, the old poet had climbed onto the dais after Marian Anderson sang her hymn to the nation. Frost had recited Scott's favorite poem, "The Gift Outright," just before the president took his oath of office. But the president's speech had been more stirring than any poem ever written. "I do not believe that any of us would exchange places with any other people or any other generation. The energy, the faith, the devotion that we bring to this endeavor will light our country and all who serve it—and the glow from that fire can truly light the world. And so, my fellow Americans: ask not what your country can do for you—ask what you can do for your country." The words "and the glow from that fire can truly light the world" could have been written by Robert Frost.

Scott wandered in the Glendale neighborhood until he came to the Wenstone Bookstore at the corner of 51st Street and Van Buren. He hid the books under his windbreaker and entered the store trying to look as casual as possible. Once inside, he introduced himself to the bookstore owner and started a conversation, thinking to get on the man's good side. He brought up Faulkner's death, which was still fresh news, believing it would engage the bookseller's interest. He said a few words in praise of Faulkner, then asked the man what he thought could be learned from his books. A short man with an ascetic face and round glasses perched on his forehead, the bookseller made a few laconic comments about Faulkner while continuing to read his magazine. When Scott asked who Faulkner's heirs might be, the man said that was a question for Faulkner's family, but he might also check the second shelf on the fiction wall under H for Heller, Joseph Heller. You could say *Catch 22* was a contemporary version of *Absalom! Absalom!* Was it an act of homage or of plagiarism? Let the reader decide. As Scott made his way to the bookcase, the bookseller spoke to his retreating back: "Nice windbreaker, young man, too bad it's a bit tight at the waist." Scott kept his composure, controlling his fear, when the front door suddenly screeched open. Footsteps pounded on the floor. Scott thought the county sheriff had come to arrest him. A voice called out, "Hello, Charlie, how're you doing?" The bookseller said, "How do you expect me to be doing? Krushchev's missiles are about to fall on our heads. The Apocalypse is scheduled for tomorrow. And what did we ever do to deserve punishment? All we wanted was to spread good around the world, and we spilled our blood for it. So where did we fall short? We have to ask ourselves what we're living for. I thought the answer was in books, but I was wrong. Maybe the answer is in the air we breathe, in the beauty of our women, the pride of our sons, the memory of our childhoods? You asked me once what book I'd bring to a desert island. I'll give you my answer, Bill, as the oldest bookseller in town: not Shakespeare, not Pound, not Hawthorne, not even the Bible. Books diverted me from life. Books are the product of pain, and they transmit pain. Don't look for life in books. Life is everywhere but in books."

"You're just saying that because you're all riled up. Maybe we're about to die, but that's no reason to revile everything we've loved! The works of Whitman, of Sinclair Lewis— they've made us the men we are."

"I've lost my faith in it, Bill. Look at the bookshelves. We've buried Hemingway and Faulkner. Dashiell Hammett, Richard Wright, and Horace McCoy are all gone, and look who's coming to take their place: Richard Stern, J. D. Salinger, Philip Roth,

Allen Ginsberg, Nabokov, Grace Paley. They're going to revive America's conscience? Neurosis, that's the only word they know how to write. Do you think Ezra Pound and Ernest Hemingway were neurotic? These New York writers can only talk about *me*. But American literature is about *us!* Papa understood that. Our literature is about the knowledge of transcendence, about baptism and redemption! The great novel is dead, Bill, and it isn't those New York writers hunched over their egos that are going to bring it back to life. The best thing to hope for is that the whole charade will end soon."

"Who knows, Charlie. If the Lord spares us, the next election may put Nixon in the White House in place of the degenerate who's there now. America may yet find new Eliots and Whitmans. *Toil on heroes! harvest the products!*

"The Mother of All, with dilated form and lambent eyes! What worries me a little, Bill, is that Nixon has never cracked a book. But at least he's not neurotic."

While the two talked, Scott, hidden from their sight, put the books back in their proper places. On the way out, he felt like a thief who has pulled off a heist. His emotions stirred, he found himself impressed with his own daring, a heady sensation.

At the corner of Glenwood and Richmond, Scott took the bus for Rolder. A moment later, he watched Phoenix recede slowly with the setting sun behind it. Darkness was falling on the plain. In the distance, peaks and ridges stood out against the sky, statues turned toward the long night. The hilltops undulated as far as the eye could see in the spectral light of a rising moon. The world's splendor gleamed in the shadow of the great rocks. He took *The Story of the Sioux* from his bookbag and picked up his reading where he'd left off.

VI

Dropped off at the Rolder stop, Scott walked home along Route 17. A breath of wind whispered fragments of song in the evening calm. From time to time the crystalline laughter of lynx or coyote would erupt from the hills. Scott looked at the sky. He balanced on the rippling glow, danced among the stars, scanned the horizon and saw nothing that was sad, bitter, or dismal, the night had conquered all that had been day. He gazed on the place where he'd grown up, where it had all started and where nothing came to an end, where he and Mom, tomorrow and for their whole life, would meet every day, where she would step out of the enormous brightness, the traces of her presence still hanging in the air, since the wind never erases her footprint, he smelled her perfume in the flood of scents floating down from the hills, his mother's scent, a bit dry, a bit strong, infiltrated the wavering shadows of the evening, accompanied him to every place on earth, this scent imprinted on the air we breathe, slipping the length of the valley on this tender October evening, where no war will come to disturb the universe and disrupt the world, nothing will ever break the established order, meeting the bus in the morning, taking a Sunday walk, enjoying solemn communion, praying hand in hand, and Mike would join him as the blue shadow of night fell across the plain, to live adventures, tell of wild escapades, relate further tales of his father's exploits, since fathers are valiant, accomplish acts of bravery, perform a thousand feats, show their sons the road, the road of night with its nodding stars, the road of day with its blazing light, they reveal the passions, give their eldest a look of triumph, dispel the phantoms of night, survive the ashes of the passing years. He walked in the midst of the procession, and the road continued on past Rolder, past Phoenix, beyond Colorado, far behind the mountains.

He reached the outskirts of town. He walked along the sidewalks. The houses were lighting up as he walked past. Inside, people were active. Children wailed. He crossed Lincoln Avenue, took Dylan Road, then found himself drawn, as he walked down Roosevelt Street, to the smell of grilling meats coming from the kitchen at Duby's. He decided to stop there for a meal.

Sitting at the counter, Scott blushed when Jenny, the waitress, came to take his order. He asked for a hamburger and a Pepsi, then kept his eyes lowered when the girl came back with his food a few minutes later. Every time she stood in front of him, Scott felt the same vague confusion. It wasn't her beauty or anything she talked about. It was more that the girl emanated a wild and ever so slightly depraved sensuality. When he was near her, he felt the same guilty rapture he felt at the sight of the erotic magazines piled up in his cousin Mike's room.

That day, Jenny was wearing the regulation uniform for Duby's, a red skirt and a blue short-sleeved shirt. The top two buttons of her shirt were undone, in defiance of the employee dress code. Her hair, which usually fell to her shoulders, was swept up in a bun. Her lipstick was big, bigger than her lips. She leaned toward him, looked him in the eyes, and said: "Scott, I've wanted to ask you this question for a long time. You've seen Elvis dance, right? So, do you know that you do the same thing with your hips? I'm positive you're not even aware you're doing it. And you're really seductive, you know that, don't you? And it's not a question of age, they say that Elvis had his first encounter when he was eight, with a prostitute. Have you ever been to a prostitute? With your angel face, I'd prefer it if you spent your money at Duby's, because, where I'm concerned, that's not something you pay for. Hey, don't think I make advances to all the guys who pass through this crummy diner and look me over as if I was a piece of meat. You're the only one I could maybe go on a romp with, because with anyone else I'd be cheating on Ted, my fiancé, and being faithful is a sacred thing, but you don't want to shut the door on pleasure either, have you ever opened the door to pleasure? Look, I've got the keys, here, at the third button, you're blushing aren't you, you're even cuter when you blush, it makes you look dazed, you look like Ted when he's undressing me, otherwise your eyes are very deep, very sensual, like Elvis again, you know they say that the King had a baby when he was 13, maybe it was you, ask your mother, of course don't say anything to your father, the last time I saw him, your old man, he'd just pushed his fist into Jack Duby's face for serving watered down gin. Watered down gin! As if that was the kind of thing they do around here. He's a little different, your dad, not that I'm saying he's bad or that the liquor old Jack serves is always the best. I'll sometimes watch your father when I'm at the counter, he sips his gin in silence, at the table in the back, and from time to time he'll slip a coin into the jukebox, I'll bet you don't know his favorite song, it's "Come Fly With Me" by Frank Sinatra and there's also "High Hopes," he's deep down sentimental, your dad, though you wouldn't think it, OK, Sinatra's not really my style, you already know that I'm an Elvis fan, do or die, and anyway your dad is pretty much ancient history around here on account of Jack Duby's broken nose, your old man has got a violent streak, not that you're gonna learn that from me, I noticed about a month ago that you had a black eye, I mean, sometimes a connection will be obvious, even to a slightly ditsy waitress, no, I know my limits, but it doesn't necessarily make you a better person to be more intelligent, you only have to look at Lyndon Jackson who has nasty written all over his face, hey, I know what I've got going for me too, a woman is a package, a whole range of things, you're going to learn that over time, because I think you're going to have a lot of women throwing themselves at you, you can tell from an early age, guys like you who always look as though they're somewhere else, we like that, no idea why, and then we end up with guys like Ted who always give the impression of being there, which gets tedious sometimes, OK you're done with your hamburger, I see you don't drag your feet, which is good, at least if you want to take your first bite of the apple with me, since Ted is stationed at Fort Lewis, Washington, for another three months, and it's not really cheating since he'll never learn about it, the whole unfaithfulness thing is in your head anyway, fifty cents for a tip, you're handsome and you're generous, hey, don't stay away, come back soon, angel face."

He went out, unsettled by Jenny's words. Was her offer serious, or had the girl been making fun of him? And what if the news ever reached Ted? He knew Ted, a giant with a heart of gold. And Ted was a Marine. America was on the point of going to war. Troops were mustering in Florida. The president was due to give a speech that very evening on a matter of the highest importance. The president was addressing the nation. October 22, 1962 might turn out to be an important date in history. Ted would be on high alert at Fort Lewis. Looking at Jenny was already an assault on the morale of the troops, responding to her would make him a traitor to America. He stopped in front of the window of Bob's Shoes, watched himself walk back and forth, inspected his reflection. There was nothing, either in his movements or in his face, that suggested Elvis's looks or his hip-swinging stance.

He walked in the half-light, through gray deserted streets. Within him, he felt a worry growing. The image of the rifle pointed at his father flashed into his mind. He recalled the icy fury of the targeted man. The whole scene replayed in his head, the oaths of unremitting hatred, the savage brutality, the threat of death, the spread of chaos. It had all happened the day before. Twenty-four hours of his own life had dispelled the memory. But could his father forget a thing like that?

The hill up which Blank Street climbed was gripped in mist. A few lights, trembling in the night, glowed in the distance. Scott couldn't tell exactly which houses they came from or, if they were from his house, whether his father was home. The wind brought him distant rumblings of a storm. Everything seemed cold, hostile, charged with portent. He'd seen the town, now he was alone. The solitude, which he normally valued, terrified him. Who reaches out a hand to us at our lowest ebb?

He clearly saw a halo of light coming from a window in his house. His father was at home. He couldn't possibly have erased from his mind the gun trained on him. A lifetime wouldn't be enough for that, its Sundays filled with prayer, petitions for absolution, requests for mercy. The image of the gun barrel wouldn't sink into the deep pit of sleep that drunkenness brings on. The gesture of defiance would never fade into oblivion. War had ravaged his father's brain, destroyed the mechanism of his feelings, switched off his emotional core, left a pile of rubble where his heart should be. But war had left the cogwheels of memory intact. Anger would blast Scott the moment he came through the door.

He had defied the ancient law of man, threatened his own progenitor with death. His crime was too great to be forgiven. He now had to answer for his offense. His father had been the victim, his father would be the prosecutor. The fact of coming to his mother's aid would not weigh in his favor. His penalty would be commuted to corporal punishment. He was used to being beaten. He had been a battered child from birth.

He wasn't sure what posture to take before his judge. Should he maintain some semblance of dignity? Should he go in with his head bowed, bent forward, offering one cheek and then the other, should he say something by way of appeasement, humbly wish his father good evening a few hours after having sworn to kill him?

He found himself in the middle of Los Lobos. Cascading laughter, a hubbub of happy voices drifted from the houses and chased away the threatening specters that prowled the street during the day. It was dinnertime. The silhouettes of women cast shadows against the windows. All that was rough and aggressive had disappeared. What mystery was this? Where would the lively murmur be gone tomorrow? Who, at daybreak, stifled the laughter and allowed the clamor to swell?

He walked, his eyes fixed on the distant glow, as an insect flies toward its fate. I'm coming toward you, Father, I know that I've committed a fault. He felt his heart beat and his temples pound. His father's past abuse of him echoed in the darkness. The stars above had deserted him. The forces of night seemed to gather in this sad place. It is written, Lord. I expect neither consolation nor support.

He entered the gate, walked through the garden and across the porch, stood in front of the door. He held his breath, turned the key slowly in the lock. The living room was in shadow. At the far end, the television screen cast a wan light. He took a step forward and saw his father sprawled on the couch, his boots on the coffee table, his hand clutching a can of Pelfort, his eyes glued to the screen. He took another step. His father's eyes stared straight ahead. Another step. Nothing happened. It was as if he didn't exist. His steps didn't creak on the floorboards, his breathing made no sound, his skin gave off no scent, the wind hadn't entered with him when the door swung open, he was reduced to nothing. Can a person who no longer exists in his father's eyes expect anything from the world? He was a ghost in the middle of the living room. He took another step and still nothing happened. Jeffrey Hatford was watching his favorite TV program, the Ted Mack Hour on CBS. Singers, magicians, and acrobats performed their numbers to a variously receptive audience. He felt guilty for his father's silence. Looking to redeem himself, he said "Hello." His greeting provoked no response. To him, I am dead. He went on to his room, a shadow among shadows, nothing left to fear, nothing more that life could do to him, but he had gone missing, a victim of adversity and misfortune. Sitting on his bed, he hesitated between relief and terror. He might escape his father's anger, he might avoid a beating, elude punishment, bypass questions about his offense. But he was no longer anyone's son. He lay down. The sound of the world reached him faintly from the living room. The Ted Mack Hour was interrupted. A news anchor spoke, it was Walter Cronkite, his voice more solemn than usual. Something serious was happening, an event such as the United States had seen only once before in its history, twenty years earlier, when the Japanese attacked Pearl Harbor, yes, what was happening was on that scale, a life-or-death threat, maybe Pearl Harbor was a bad example, maybe nothing in our past could match the horror of what we were witnessing now, this entirely new tragedy in the history of America and in the history of humanity, the specter of nuclear holocaust, the danger that the world would end. In every house there had to be great fear, in every mind. This was a terrible moment. It was time to listen to the president, John Fitzgerald Kennedy was now going to address the nation.

"Good evening my fellow citizens. This government, as promised, has maintained the closest surveillance of the Soviet military buildup on the island of Cuba." The president's voice rose into the night, reverberated in the room, and warmed Scott's heart. "Within the past week, unmistakable evidence has established the fact that a series of offensive missile sites is now in preparation on that imprisoned island. The purpose of these bases can be none other than to provide a nuclear strike capability against the Western Hemisphere." The president spoke in a firm voice, a voice that knew how to find words, calm fears. "Upon receiving the first preliminary hard information of this nature last Tuesday morning at 9 a.m., I directed that our surveillance be stepped up. And having now confirmed and completed our evaluation of the evidence and our decision on a course of action, this government feels obliged to report this new crisis to you in fullest detail." There was no tremor in his voice, which was the triumphant voice of America, flush with courage and inflected with wisdom. "The characteristics of these new missile sites indicate two distinct types of installations. Several of them include medium-range ballistic missiles capable of carrying a nuclear warhead for a distance of more than 1,000 nautical miles. Each of these missiles, in short, is capable of striking Washington, D. C., the Panama Canal, Cape Canaveral, Mexico City, or any other city in the southeastern part of the United States, in Central America, or in the Caribbean area." Suddenly the voice went silent. There was a muffled crackling. The television set, bought a year earlier in a pawnshop on Capitol Street for a few dollars and subject to frequent breakdowns, had stopped receiving. After a long interruption while Jeffrey Hatford twiddled the dials and repositioned the antennas, President Kennedy resumed. "The 1930's taught us a clear lesson: aggressive conduct, if allowed to go unchecked and unchallenged, ultimately leads to war." Scott silently repeated the president's words: "Aggressive conduct, if allowed to go unchecked and unchallenged, ultimately leads to war." He looked at the photograph of JFK tacked to his wall. He had the impression the president was talking directly to him. "Aggressive conduct leads to war." How could the president be so right about everything, explain the world, and also talk about Jeffrey Hatford?

In these terrible days, the president knew the right words to say because he had already been through the worst. On the night of August 1, 1943, when PT 109, the patrol torpedo boat he commanded, was sunk by a Japanese ship, JFK ordered his men to cling to the burning wreckage. JFK towed one of the wounded men through the water with his teeth clamped to the strap of the man's life vest. JFK steered his men to Plum Island, held by the Japanese. After several days without food or water, JFK led the castaways to safety. He saved his men from drowning and hunger, he'll save the American people from the shipwreck that threatened. "I have directed that the following steps be taken immediately: first, to halt this offensive buildup, a strict quarantine on all offensive military equipment under shipment to Cuba is being initiated. All ships of any kind bound for Cuba from whatever nation or port will, if found to contain cargoes of offensive weapons, be turned back. This quarantine will be extended, if needed, to other types of cargo and…" The voice went silent again, replaced by a crackling sound. Jeffrey Hatford started swearing, accused the Soviets, the Mexicans, the Negroes, the Jews, and every politician in Washington of interfering with his reception, of plotting against him. The sofa creaked, the floorboards groaned. The sound of boots came from the living room, then entered the hallway. The footsteps came nearer, and Scott's fear increased. He thought of the president. He should follow JFK's example. Walk in his footsteps. Not raise his voice. Not succumb to panic. Remain in control of himself, master his fears. Not incite anger. Not provoke by his presence. Not count the minutes, or the hours. Want nothing from nightfall, want nothing from daybreak. Not make a display of himself, but go into concealment, squelch his anguish, his rebellion, his pain, even the beating of his heart. Grow hard, turn to marble, hold still, stop his breathing, stifle his tears at the source, take to darkness, take to shadow. Bite his lips, not cry. Accept the law of men, unlearn justice, forget what's true, or great, or aglow with beauty. Go into eclipse, melt into space, melt into the silence of forests, beam himself to a distant land in the heart of a great and wondrous country, walk empty-handed, his face streaming with insults, own the courage to be nothing, discard his strength, his hopes, his sorrows, leave this endless day, sink into sleep, wake at dawn, cover himself with suffering, avoid looking or listening, wrap himself in mystery, hate life, turn to stone, withdraw from the world, race along the precipice, roam among the angels, make himself invisible, forgotten. Disappear.

His father's shape filled the doorway, as quiet as if he were waiting in ambush. Then the man entered and stood by the bed, his shadow cast onto the wall between the crucifix and the president's photograph. Stay calm before this angry face, show no expression that could be taken for defiance or provocation.

"Did you monkey with the television set?"

Scott said no.

"Stand when I talk to you."

Scott stood.

"Lower your eyes in your father's presence!"

He looked the man in the eye. The first slap landed.

"Listen to your father."

He made no motion. A second slap. He lowered his eyes.

"Look at me when I talk to you!"

He kept his eyes on the ground. A third slap. He raised his head.

"You wanted to kill me yesterday?"

He didn't feel guilty of any crime. He expressed no remorse, offered no excuse. He didn't justify himself, explain his intentions.

"Someday I'm going to kill you, you and your mother both, then I'll put a bullet through my own head... Unless you'd prefer that I start at the end?"

He was ordered to answer. Blows rained down on him. He could feel his determination waver. He looked at the crucifix on the wall. O Heavenly Lord, You are my salvation and my faith.

His father insisted that he kneel and ask for mercy. He stayed standing, saying nothing. I kneel only to the Lord. You're not the master of the world. You're not the master of me. The man who oversees the progress of the world asks no one to bow down before him. For a few moments, his mind turned completely to the photograph of John F. Kennedy. He remembered the pictures of the president and his family. JFK on a sailboat with his children. JFK at the tiller. JFK lifting his son in his arms, dancing with his daughter. JFK smiled at Jackie the way he smiled at the world: and the world smiled back at him. JFK was a model father and a model American. JFK embodied all of America, from pioneers to soldiers, this country's men and its children, the American Dream, America's storied past.

Jeffrey Hatford saw that Scott wasn't paying full attention to him. He turned toward the wall. He reached for the crucifix, then changed his mind, went to the photo of JFK, snatched it, tore it up.

"You're not to post any more photos of this agent of socialism, this traitor to the nation."

He threw the bits of paper on the ground.

Scott was a dog, his mother a whore. He was the son of a whore. Lord, protect me from anger, protect me from hatred. His father slapped him again and he felt blood running at the back of his mouth.

"You find this funny? You're going to stand up to me?"

Scott wondered if a glimmer of contempt might have slipped into his eyes. He wanted his eyes to turn off. He wanted everything in him to turn off. Lord, master of miracles, make me invisible to my father. Make me a shadow, turn me to dust.

His father unbuckled his belt. Scott knew what this meant, he turned around, pulled down his pants. The blows rained down. The belt buckle left vivid marks on his upper buttocks. He looked at the crucifix. Lord, in hating the author of my days, am I not hating You too? Perhaps God was testing him. His father was only the messenger, an angel carrying out the will of heaven—the exterminating angel.

"You're going to respect me, do you understand?"

His father had no respect for persons. Lord, how can one of your creatures thrash another, a father thrash his son until he draws blood? What kind of man was his father? What kind of father was Jeffrey Hatford?

The belt kept lashing his back. He collapsed to the ground. The beating stopped. The toes of his father's boots were in front of him, the pointed tips a few inches from his face, threatening to crush him. From the ground, his father's legs seemed to rise forever, their shadow across the floor enormous. His father was an evil giant, a colossus in leather boots, an abject creature, a child-devouring ogre, a triumphant tyrant. The boots took a step backward, the left boot more slowly than the right. The threat was receding. The heels turned. The boots moved away with a creaking sound. The shadow was withdrawing. The legs moved toward the doorway, one leg dragging. The door closed.

He stayed sprawled, motionless, his eyes on the doorway, afraid the shadow would reappear, loom over him again. The door stayed shut. A voice cursed on the far side of the wall. He heard the sound of a body collapsing onto the sofa. He did not move, his head against the floor. Despite the pain, he felt good. He hadn't really cried. He hadn't capituled to his father's demands. He hadn't been intimidated when his father unbuckled his belt. He hadn't screamed during the beating. No curses had passed his lips. He'd respected the commandment to respect his father. He'd stayed a good Christian. He felt guilty of nothing.

He looked at the pieces of the photograph scattered on the floor. He collected them one by one, removed a tube of glue and a piece of paper from a drawer, sat at his desk. He spread the glue across the paper, laid out the torn fragments. He had a puzzle in front of him whose subject was a face. He assembled the mouth and cheeks, found the left eye and the right, put the nose in the middle, replaced the bits of forehead where they belonged. The president's face was once more whole. He smoothed the sheet of paper. There. John F. Kennedy was smiling at him again.

He looked at JFK's face. He wondered if the president had had feelings of hatred toward his father, Joseph. He'd read a whole book on Joseph Kennedy—and everything else in the school library about the Kennedys. What he remembered was that Joe Kennedy was a despicable man, driven by ambition, blinded by his hatred of Jews, unprincipled, ignorant of ethics and scornful of morality, who liked Hitler over Roosevelt. How could such a bastard be the father of this exemplary man, this world hero, the man who lighted our path? Had the president one day rebelled against Joe, had he considered, for a fraction of a second, killing his father? The book didn't say.

VII

Clinking sounds came from the kitchen. The refrigerator door opened and shut. Grease sizzled in a pan. Glasses and plates were being set down on the kitchen table. The smell of bacon tickled his nose. His mother's voice called him to get out of bed and stop lollygagging. She'd made breakfast. He should hurry. They were already late for church.

From her cheerful voice, he knew that his father had already left. On Sunday, the man made it a point of honor to leave the house before Mom got back from her night shift.

He stretched and looked out the window. The blue sky glowed with the pure bounty of existence. The Lord's day was a day of rejoicing.

"Get out of bed, darling one! Or the pastor will scold us again!"

He felt a stab of pain in his lower back, remembered the day before, the shouts of hatred, the hard blows raining on him. He slipped into the bathroom, looked at himself in the mirror, and was relieved to find that his face had no mark of the blows he'd received. The scars striping his buttocks made no difference. Once he had his shirt on, Mom wouldn't know a thing.

"Would you pick out a dress for me, dear?" said his mother from the kitchen.

He pulled on his clothes, then went into her bedroom, opened wide the closet, hesitated between various outfits, and finally chose a flounced dress that came to mid-calf, which he placed on the bed, before entering the kitchen. A minute or two later, his mother returned, stood in front of him, and twirled in place. "Do I look nice? Not easy considering the dress you picked for me." What did she have against the dress? "It's the one dress I still have of my mother's. And I suspect that she got it from her mother." He drank his orange juice, ate his bacon. "You think any dress that only comes to the knee should be banned." He didn't understand. She bent over and covered him with kisses. "My little gentleman doesn't follow?" She burst out laughing.

He turned up the sound of the transistor radio on the table and listened. The news announcer was talking about the missile crisis. A gust of panic was blowing through America. Grocery stores were being emptied of their goods as Americans stockpiled food. Gasoline would soon be in short supply. Senator Capehart accused President Kennedy of being soft on Cuba in his televised address and argued for annihilating the island immediately.

"Mom, what will we do if there is a war?"

"Nothing is going to happen."

"Did you hear Senator Capehart?"

"Indiana never chooses its representatives very sensibly. President Kennedy knows what he is doing."

He pricked the yolk of an egg, sopped it up. Then why were they performing those drills at school? They'd been taught how to put on gas masks that were too big and slipped off their foreheads, squashed their noses, made it impossible to breathe. They'd practiced lining up by twos and evacuating the classroom, staying calm. An officer in the reserves had explained to them how to shelter under a desk if an atomic bomb exploded, what position to adopt, the best way to curl up.

"People like to scare each other."

He looked up admiringly at his mother. She hadn't stockpiled any food. She wasn't worried about tomorrow. Nuclear missiles,

Krushchev, his father—none of them frightened her. His mother was afraid of nothing and no one.

"Drink your orange juice!" she said, making him jump. "Pastor Simpson is going to banish us from his church if we arrive late again!"

#

They walked through town, the two of them, side by side, she leaning on him and slowing his steps. The heat of the morning swirled around them. A blond light filled the air. The sunny mist, the valley that cradled Rolder, the mountains, and beyond the mountain tops, beyond the deserts, the great open prairie, the proud cities rising to the sky, the savage strength of rivers, the forests of big elms, the deep trenches in the ocean, the moons that rose over sleeping forests, everything belonged to them, proclaimed the boundless miracle of time, raised psalms to the eternity of the moment, watched over the life they shared, and the silvery peaks of New Mexico, the golden valleys of California, the lush grass of the Potomac Valley, the springtime torrents of Arkansas, the deepwater bays of the Mississippi celebrated the grandeur and the glory of this morning, which no wounded soul, cruel and unhappy, came to intrude on, and the morning's vastness that devoured space sang words of peace at daybreak.

On Capitol Street, they passed Mr. and Mrs. Brown. He was working under the hood of his old Buick, while his wife watched. Mr. Brown raised his head and said, "I finally found the problem! It's the starter. Tonight, Scott, this old beauty will be cruising down Route 66."

"Don't listen to him, Mrs. Hatford," said Mrs. Brown. "The day that jalopy starts driving again, the skies will rain down ducks and geese. Scott, it's good to see you walking quietly... You hold his arm tight, Mrs. Hatford, or he'll fly away. Don't you let him run off the way I let my Johnny run off. You remember my son John, don't you? When I worked at the post office, he was always right behind the counter with me. But I let Johnny fly away. Luckily, I still have his letters. He wrote me every day when he was in Korea. I keep them carefully, those letters, in a vase away from sunlight, it's all I have left of him. One day, I carried the whole stack to the post office to weigh them, twelve and a half ounces! When you think that he weighed just short of ten pounds when he was born! Ten pounds when he came from the womb, and twelve and a half ounces twenty years later... When Johnny enlisted, his sergeant told me that the army turned boys into men! But Johnny wasn't like your Scott, he never could run fast. What he loved was chess. I'd tell him, Stop playing chess, what good will it ever do you in this life? They never listen to their mother! To their sergeant, who orders them to charge a minefield, sure! You know, they didn't even find his dogtag afterwards! They didn't want to go into a lot of detail when they came to bring me the news. They do that well, they're very professional, very respectful of people.

They take the time to explain it to you, you'll see, you have a son, no complaints on that score. One fine day, they ring your doorbell, standing there in their nice uniforms. You know the moment you open the door. You might have been stupid enough to put your son's life in their hands, but you haven't completely lost your marbles. All the same, they walk you through the formalities. They wear a solemn expression—it must be their idea of how you're supposed to look at a funeral. They go on as if your son had saved the United States of America, when you know that all the idiot did was put his foot where he shouldn't have, even though you've been telling him to be careful since he was born. They maintain their composure, their dignity, you serve them something to drink, you're almost hoping that they'll spend the afternoon with you except you know they've got more bad news to deliver. They don't spend an eternity with you. They let you have eternity to yourself. That feeling of emptiness you feel when they go out the door, that's a present from your country. Not that I blame them, a job like that can't be fun, day after day. But that's what shows how a great a nation we are, the protocol they follow in telling you that they never found a trace of your son's insides. You don't open the front door the same way after that, believe me. But it doesn't matter much, you know it will never be your son John standing on the welcome mat. But you know all this, your husband was in Korea, even if it was only his leg that was damaged. Although he seems to have taken some shrapnel to the brain too… At any rate, it wasn't all for nothing. Just think, if my son and your husband had not gone there to fight, the Chinese would have crossed the 38th parallel! That's what comforts me on days when my Johnny's absence hurts too much and even his letters don't console me. I think about the 38th parallel. And then I start writing my youngest, Tom, who isn't afraid of the Chinese and who enlisted to get revenge for his brother. We have a strong sense of honor in this family. Tom was supposed to go to Vietnam to punish the guilty party. But with this missile crisis, maybe they'll send him to Cuba, even if the Cubans and the Chinese are not exactly the same thing, and when Cuba's over, they'll send our boys to Saigon. Then Tom can have the scalps of the slant-eyed enemy who killed his brother. All I hope is that I won't see those two guys in uniform on my doorstep one morning in place of Tom. I'm not sure I could stand it a second time... But I'm boring you with my talk of war. Goodbye, Mrs. Hatford. And Scott, keep training to run fast, in five or six years your country is going to need you!"

A long silence followed, then Mom made Scott solemnly promise never to enlist in the army. He said his father had served in two wars. Your father, she answered, is not a good example. Scott had to agree. "If the U.S. is still at war when you turn 18, I'm going to send you to live with my uncle in Ireland." She didn't want him to go into battle, not against the Russians, not against the Chinese. She couldn't care less about Krushchev. Some day, Krushchev would die, Mao would die, Castro would be assassinated, even President Kennedy would pass away. But she and Scott would still be alive. That was the important thing. Her son wouldn't go to war for any number of victories. Teaching Cuba a lesson, showing Vietnam a thing or two? She didn't even know where Saigon was on the map. Did he know where Saigon was? He nodded. She instructed him to forget it. "How can I do that?" She repeated her request. He shut his eyes, concentrated. He had forgotten.

"Good, that's my angel."

#

Pastor Simpson was waiting for them in front of the church, a wooden building constructed in the nineteenth century and recently renovated by the town.

"Here you are, finally! You know I waited for you last week?"

Mom apologized and explained that she had had a long night at the hospital.

"You're forgiven. Bringing bodies back to health is more taxing work than shepherding souls. And Meredith Hatford doesn't need to pray to the Lord. It's the Lord who needs Meredith Hatford."

Scott asked Pastor Simpson whether the mayor would be in church that morning.

"Our mayor believes that restoring the facade of the church is ample payment for his sins. Our mayor prefers to sleep late on Sunday mornings."

Scott questioned Pastor Simpson about a certain Elizabeth Lloyd, an assistant at town hall with whom he was corresponding. Did the pastor know this lady? Did she come to church?

"I know all the citizens of this town, including the Jews and the Negroes. But I don't know Elizabeth Lloyd. Why?"

Scott said nothing. Pastor Simpson urged them to enter the church. The service was about to start. They slipped inside and took a seat in the fourth row, near Mr. and Mrs. Hawlin, who greeted them with a nod. The service started. They recited the Nicene Creed, sang the Agnus Dei, the Doxology. The pastor told the parable of the good Samaritan. They sang again. Then the pastor said: "Dear children of mine, dear children of the Lord, this is not a time for laughter or lightheartedness. I know that this time is still the time, that this place of our prayer is still the place. But the season of lilacs springing from the ground, of hyacinths overflowing our cup is past. Our Earth has given us what it had to give. An icy wind is soon to sweep through Heaven. Grant us thy peace, O Lord. The minions of the Foul Fiend have aimed their rockets at America. The hour of the Apocalypse seems at hand. The nation has sinned, we have challenged Heaven. We have provoked the Godhead, unleashed his wrath and his vengeance. For it is not Krushchev who installed missiles in Cuba, but Our Lord. The Creator will punish us, raise His vengeful arm against us. Humankind is earmarked for destruction. Man has sinned, and the most powerful man is the first among sinners. Nothing of the dreams of the pioneers remains. The sacred poem that once rose up from Earth no longer drifts heavenward. Evil has sullied man's body and perverted his soul. Men lie, steal, and wallow in debauchery. Men leave the valley to build cities. Men lie with other men. The earth is plundered and destroyed. Whatever the joint chiefs and the president may say, the day is coming when no light will shine. God has given, God will take away, blessed be His name. See the weapons of death that the Reds have installed within a stone's throw of our nation. And the barbarous army units marching through Moscow. The Fiend hides under those uniforms. The Communists are the cruelest men. The world they depict is a world without God, soulless and loveless. They believe in Man, they believe in nothing. They are without faith or law. Nothing horrifies them, nothing frightens them. They will sow destruction over the land and in every heart. And who will protect us, I ask you, except Our Lord? Our president? We have chosen the worst of men to lead us. A man unworthy of commanding America, a Catholic, more devoted to the pope than to our sacred country. The blood in his veins is the blood of a depraved man. The whispers, the rumors that swirl around him are only a drop in the ocean of truth. Krushchev and Kennedy are two facets of one Evil. Plague and cholera. The man watching over our fate is intent on defending the rights of men whose skin is of a different color, men that God did not designate as our equals, men who do not share our blood. He lives in a cauldron of lust, surrounded by perverts and members of the race that crucified Our Lord. How can such a man save America? Never will Our God whisper acts of courage in his ear, or suggest to him ideas that might save us. May God lead us back to the path that He laid out for us, the path of faith, of morality. May our president be struck by grace or removed definitively from office. May God watch over America, the land of freedom and justice. Lord have mercy on us sinners. Amen."

The congregation answered "Amen." And while the choirboys were blowing out the candles, Scott asked his mother if the pastor was not exaggerating about the president and the Apocalypse.

"You're right, sweetheart. There will be no Apocalypse. God is watching over us."

"And over President Kennedy?"

"God is also watching over the president."

They exited the church, pausing briefly on the steps to greet a few friends. Then they left.

#

She wanted to have lunch at Duby's. He claimed he didn't feel like a hamburger. She said she was hungry. They crossed Virginia Street and walked to the restaurant, which they found empty. They chose a table, and Jenny came to take their order, an ironic smile playing at the corners of her lips.

"Now then, what would my first customers of the day (and probably my last) like to order?"

He chose a roast beef grinder with onion rings, a Coca-cola, and a banana split for dessert. Mom ordered a chicken salad and a coffee. When Jenny left, Mom asked Scott if he knew the girl. He blushed and shook his head.

"At your age, the girls are going to start noticing you."

He wasn't interested in girls.

"You'll change your mind, Scott. Some day, there will be girls hanging around in front of our door."

"Do you think any girl with half a brain would climb that hill?"

"Elizabeth Taylor will climb the hill to see you."

"Elizabeth Taylor is old."

"She's ten years younger than I am."

Jenny returned, served their dishes, and said, "Can you believe it? It's a Sunday and you're my only customers. What's wrong with everybody? Do they think the Commies are going to attack Duby's?" She turned and went back behind the counter.

He grabbed his sandwich with both hands, ate two big bites, wiped his mouth. Mom tasted her salad and said, "Fear makes people crazy. But fear also makes them take a step back. You'll see, Krushchev is going to be afraid of President Kennedy, the Russians will go away."

He drank his Coke, attacked his plate of fried onions, raised his head, asked if there was anything that made his father afraid.

"Your father is afraid of everything."

Fear was what made his anger boil over, she explained. Fear accompanied him on his drinking bouts. It prowled around him day and night. He tried to drown it in alcohol, dilute it in bourbon. But after his last glass, even his shadow scared him.

He asked whether there was a way of addressing that fear, of finding out what caused it.

"Don't bother, sweetheart, you'd be wasting your time."

Had he always been like this? Was there a time in his father's life that Scott could be proud of? A son should know those things.

"You want me to tell the story of how I met him, don't you?"

He nodded.

"I've told you ten times already. But then, it's the part of my life that you like best."

Mom's face glowed with candor. She started talking in a soft voice. From the memory of those days long past, her face registered expressions that time had erased. The grating noise of the world, the fears that rise in the night had faded away. Scott beheld his mother as she'd been before becoming his mother.

On the fourth Thursday in November, 1943, she is traveling to Boston to celebrate Thanksgiving with her family. She's on a bus from New York City, where she's been at school, and she's wearing a red wool dress with pleats. It's early afternoon, she's watching the rain come down outside the window, daydreaming as the grassy hills and the forests turned yellow and brown by the advancing autumn roll past. She feels someone next to her on her right, guesses it's a man, forces herself not to turn her head. She's cautious with men. When one of them sits next to her in the bus, she's always careful to keep a distance between them, to affect a certain detachment, not to ask questions in turn. She hasn't to this day broken these rules of caution. As soon as her neighbor starts a conversation, she makes a game of pigeonholing him in a mental category, from a list that includes the conceited, the tongue-tied, and the perverted, smart- alecks, comedians, creeps, men who pretend to be bashful, charmers, lunatics, bores, dimwits, nice guys, depressives, smooth talkers, sunshine boys, oafs, snakes in the grass, nebbishes, confidence men, ditherers, rough cobs, cheeky sausages, doormats, cynics, level heads, louts, quick thinkers, dolts, rebels, and troubled souls. You can be stupid and pretentious at the same time, perverted and funny. She hates the lotharios and the cynics. She is drawn toward those who are quiet, feels sympathetic toward those who are desperate, can't stand the ones who pretend to be shy. She looks out the window at the undulating hills, the mist-filled forests, and the small towns lashed by the rain. Suddenly, the voice of the man next to her rings in her ears. It's a warm voice, a little melancholy. The man is looking for a light.

"I'm not sure that I have one," she says.

"It's better that way."

"You mean, not to smoke?"

"No, it's better not to be sure of yourself... It's one of my problems too, I'm always unsure."

"You don't look that way."

"People fall for appearances pretty easily."

"I'm not people."

"No, of course not, you're...?"

"Meredith, Meredith Barnett."

"Pleased to meet you. Jeffrey, Jeffrey Hatford."

She shakes the hand he holds out to her. Wanting to hide her confusion, she looks out the window again, lets the silence settle between them. The countryside has lost its charm. The parade of forests and lakes strikes her as monotonous. She finds herself hoping the conversation will continue. The impulse makes her ashamed. She closes her eyelids. What would her father think if he could see his daughter aching for a stranger to address her? The man picks up the conversational thread, congratulates her for not smoking. She dismisses her father and opens her eyes. They say it isn't good for your health. Even if the Marlboro Man looks perfectly fit. She looks at him intently. Does he ever get around to talking seriously?

"If I'm ever serious, I get sad."

She doesn't dislike sad people.

"Lucky you... What do you do for a living?"

She wants to become a nurse.

"Are you drawn towards desperate cases?"

She turns away, annoyed. This one is a lothario and a pervert together. He joins all the hated categories in one person. He is the worst kind of man. With the gentle pressure of his hand on her chin, he brings her face toward him.

"I ship for Europe in a week," he says. "I'd like to see you when I get back."

She feels her emotions well up in her. No one has ever dealt with her in this way, made her turn her head just by moving his index finger.

"You're one of the rare good reasons for coming back from a war."

She nods without exactly knowing what she is agreeing to. She doesn't say another word. She is afraid of betraying her thoughts. She watches him while he ferrets in his pockets for something to write with. He holds a pencil and paper out to her. She jots down her address. Abruptly he plants a kiss on her lips that she doesn't have time to avoid. Just as suddenly, he rises from his seat, rushes down the aisle, asks the bus driver to stop and let him off right there. The driver complies. The man climbs off the bus. She follows him with her eyes. He is standing on the edge of the road, looking up toward her. He makes big waving motions, which she answers by blowing him a kiss.

Some twenty months later, Lieutenant Hatford rang her doorbell. It was the same man—big and strong, with a warm voice. But the sadness in the back of his eyes conveyed how much blood he had seen spilled. And the man seemed to carry the corpse of his youth draped over his shoulders.

"It's a nice story, no?"

He nodded.

She had to rush off to the hospital to fill in for Gladys Chapman, who'd called in sick. He asked if he could come along, as he had once last year. He'd enjoyed watching her pass among the patients in her white uniform, she seemed to fly. Mom said no. The hospital was not a place for a boy his age. It was no place for anyone.

"Time for me to go, angel. And don't get home too late. You have homework to do."

He had to keep being first in his class. She was proud of him. She'd be proud of him if he were the last in the whole school. He was her pride. She rose, embraced him, walked to the door, then came back on her steps and told him not to wait for her tomorrow morning at the bus stop, she would leave work later than usual and miss the first bus, as Gladys's absence was throwing all the work schedules off. She left the restaurant. He kept her in sight as she walked down the street, losing track of her when she reached a small cluster of people around a nearby drugstore.

He waved at Jenny and went out. Caught up in his mother's story and as though carried in spite of himself toward a long-ago Boston, he passed the people on the sidewalk without noticing them, agitated men and women queuing up, talking heatedly to each other, discussing the crisis in Cuba, we're headed toward war, a full-scale war people are saying, we're going to invade Cuba, the Commies will retaliate, and we'll destroy them, we need to stock up on food, flour, milk, this place has run out of vegetable oil. Scott was deaf to their grumblings, lost to the querulous voices of the men. In his mind, all was calm, silent, brimming with charm and perfection. His thoughts were roaming the East Coast. He looked through his mother's eyes. He spoke in his father's voice. He was Meredith Barnett, and he was Lieutenant Hatford. Riding a bus through green and verdant landscapes, he retraced the brief course of a budding passion, with its promise of lilting tomorrows. Trained on the horizons of New England, he felt unafraid of the night, breathed the sweet cool of the mist-shrouded hills and tasted already the first innocent day overflowing with tenderness, the intrepid assault on secret territories, promises of the unknown and the dizziness of parting. He was living through the moment when everything hangs in the balance, fortune and fate, the life one thought settled is helplessly swept away by rapturous delight and giddy hope. He savored the jubilation of the young, their immortal beauty and eternal vows, when everything is both moving quickly and poised in the moment, the future coming to fruition and the present full of grace. Is unhappiness our only fate?

VIII

He was wandering uncertainly up Dylan Road when he saw the blinking marquee of the Stuart Theater in the distance and walked toward it. At two o'clock there were showings of *Spartacus, West Side Story, Rio Bravo, Some Like It Hot*, and *A Time to Love and a Time to Die*. He hadn't seen the last two. The one with Tony Curtis and Marilyn Monroe didn't tempt him. The other was directed by Douglas Sirk, whose *Captain Lightfoot,* starring Rock Hudson, he had liked. *A Time to Love and a Time to Die* was based on a novel by Erich Maria Remarque and starred John Gavin. Scott had never understood what people saw in him. According to the publicity broadsheet next to the poster, the movie showed World War II from the vantage of the German soldiers. Since he'd been old enough to go to the movies, Scott had tried to see every film about the war. He thought it would help him understand his father. It hadn't worked till now. His father was still a mystery. Scott walked toward him as if in an eerie dream. He came back defeated and wounded in the flesh.

He hesitated whether to join the ticket line. The German perspective on the war didn't interest him. The Germans were murderers, barbarians, savages. The Germans had laid waste to the entire world. The Germans had wrecked his father, altered him to their image, made him a cruel and despicable creature. On the other hand, times had changed. Today, the devil was Soviet. The president said the Germans were allies. Berlin was on the side of freedom. Had the time come for forgiveness? If it applied to the Germans, did it also apply to his father? He stepped up to the booth and bought a ticket. The movie couldn't be any worse than the one about the bunch of dimbulbs singing their heads off in the streets of New York. He bought some popcorn and took a seat in the darkened room.

The movie lasted a little more than two hours. It was a love story between two young Germans at the end of the war. Cities were crumbling under Allied bombing. German soldiers roamed the devastated countryside in rags. In the last scene, the main character, a young Wehrmacht officer, died heroically, refusing to murder a band of Red Army soldiers. The last shot showed his fiancée's letter fluttering from his lifeless fingers. The movie left you with a bitter aftertaste. The actor looked too handsome in his uniform. Scott had never seen anything like it onscreen—a good German. For sure, his father had never crossed paths with such a noble enemy. For sure, a German like that was an invention of the movies.

It was time to head home. He crossed town and started up Blank Street. He'd hardly climbed a dozen yards before he heard voices shouting at the top of the hill. As he advanced, the noise grew louder. There was menace in the air. Spanish insults rang out. He thought it was the local kids mixing it up in front of their houses, but when he reached Los Lobos, everything was quiet. He looked in the distance. What he saw confirmed his fears. Next to his house was a tangle of kids and a few yards away his father. He had ventured out past the fence to confront the boys and was walking unsteadily down the path, hampered by his limp. Seven or eight teenagers were taunting him. The man faced the throng head-on and advanced on them. Usually when he watched his father walk, Scott felt his own leg grow weak until he, too, was limping. This time it was different. He felt great strength pour into him and wings sprout from his back. The teens surrounded his father and formed a circle around him. Scott could hear their voices more clearly now:

"Hey Gimpy-Guy, let's see you run! Go on, run, Gimp-Man!" His father lunged at one after another of the boys. His left foot scraped the dirt behind him. His hand snatched at the boys but caught only air. The kids yelled in his face, dashed up to him, slipped out of his grasp. They laughed at his confusion, this paper tiger trying to uphold his honor, as though he had honor to salvage, as though it hadn't already been worn to the nub. And the laughter spilled down the hill to pound against Scott's ears, laughter that fed on humiliation, the laughter of the many, savage barbarian peels, the laughter of bastards scenting blood and closing in for the kill, laughter steeped in drunkenness and laced with blood. He climbed the hill, sweating, chest heaving. Help me, O Lord, Father in whom we must believe. A pack of kids was tormenting his father. "*Ole!*" they chorused each time Jeffrey Hatford flailed at one of them. Scott was running, filled with a strange emotion, a mixture of sorrow and joy, shame and terror. Then he saw, yikes, his father trip in the dark, fall to the ground, bite the dust. The pack whooped with glee. It seemed the whole town re-echoed with the cry, caught the fever of the *corrida* bringing down the man who, for years, had breached the rules of society, respected nobody, challenged law and order, mocked the social contract, spat on custom, the man who deserved hanging for his offences against the family, against work, against the church, and against his country, the United States that he had served so faithfully and to which he owed everything except that one leg, but the United States didn't need Lieutenant Hatford's leg to keep its spot at the top of world rankings. His downed father let out a groan, and Scott felt his strength grow exponentially. Now the boys were circling around the man in a sinister dance, singing a savage song. Scott started to shout at them. He yelled for them to stop in a threatening voice he hardly recognized. Woe unto you! He'd beat them senseless, knock their heads together. Damnation upon you! When he was about ten yards away, they stopped their dance, turned toward him, smiled at his livid expression. Scott stopped. He saw his father on the ground, face in the dust, eyes turned toward him. One of the boys, a giant twice his size, moved to intercept him. Scott flew at him. O Lord, guide my hand, as you guided David's hand against Goliath. Scott caught the teenager by the neck, threw him to the ground, and battered him with his fists until the boy's mouth dribbled blood. He straightened, saw, horrified, the boy's face smeared with scarlet, his right eye closed, his eyelid swollen. Someone spat in his face, someone muttered. "Your father's a drunk, your mother's a whore." Scott stood up. The boys backed away. Scott turned toward his father. Lieutenant Hatford was retreating to the house. Scott followed in his father's footsteps. The teens threw rocks at them. A stone struck him on the head. He ignored the pain. He heard the words "coward," "wimp," "fairy." He didn't turn around. He tried only to keep a little distance between himself and his father. The boys threw more stones, promised they would get back at him. He crossed the threshold behind his father. He shut the door, stopped in the entryway, not daring to speak, to walk another step. He tried to understand what had happened, what his hands had managed to do, what had followed from his hatred. He had spilled blood. He could find no meaning, no comfort in his actions. Absolute silence had replaced the wild yelling. His father was sitting on a kitchen chair, his face in shadow. His face betrayed no gratitude, no sadness, no joy. Yet something important had happened out there, on the dirt track, something tangible that nothing could ever erase, that thing men call "the family bond" and which, up till now, he had always associated with his father's belt buckle. They'd shared an adventure. Together, they'd fought the Mexican-American War. They'd triumphed over a great multitude. Maybe when he saw

Scott punch the Mexican in the face, his father had thought: "My son is brave, my blood flows through his veins!" Scott waited motionless, petrified, certain that a moment of communion with his father was at hand, a moment such as he might never live again, such as each son lives only once in a lifetime. His father looked at him insistently. Maybe he was looking for the words to express his feelings? Affectionate words, charged with tenderness, were not part of his normal vocabulary. O Lord, give my father the strength to find words, and the courage to say them. In the leaden stillness of the room, his father continued to stare at him, entrenched in silence. O Lord, come to his aid, just as You multiplied my strength in facing the Mexican giant. Jeffrey Hatford stood suddenly, advanced his tall frame toward his son, anchored his gaze in Scott's, and said, "You think your father can't defend himself on his own? Your father's a cripple, right?" Scott shook his head. Jeffrey Hatford walked to his room, his foot dragging over the floor, opened the door, then turned back to say,

"You and your mother, you enjoy that, don't you, humiliating me in front of strangers?"

IX

It was about 3 p.m. when Scott stepped off the bus on Route 17. When he reached Each Ranch, he saw Ted, the youngest son, riding his horse. He waved at him and called out his name. The teenager turned his horse and walked up to the fence where Scott was standing. The horse allowed Scott to stroke its head. It was the same one that Ted had lent him last year when he was teaching him to ride.

"My father's about to break a colt. Do you want to watch?" asked Ted.

Scott thanked him but no. They spoke for a bit, then pursued their separate ways.

Scott had already seen Ted's father break a wild horse. The sight of the lasso whirling through the air to catch the horse's hind legs and the terrifying sound of the animal falling to the ground stayed in his memory. He could still see Owen Each holding the mustang by the bridge of the nose. The man covered the horse's eyes with his hands and whispered in his ear to quiet him. Within a few moments, the flat rein and the hackamore were in place. The animal, hogtied, heaved to its feet, reared, stumbled, fought out against its restraints, whinnied desperately, darted its mad eyes in all directions, and fell heavily in a cloud of dust. Scott hadn't wanted to watch any more of it.

Continuing on his way, Scott thought of the mustang cemetery, the high-headed cavalcade that sank into the sea. Why shouldn't he try to save one of those horses from drowning? Why shouldn't he wrest an animal from its fate? Thanks to Ted, he knew how to ride. He could take up a position along the East River. He'd wait until the herd came down to the beach. He'd single out the youngest mustang. He'd dash toward it through the herd. He wouldn't need any equipment. No lasso or hackamore, he'd go in barehanded. He'd straddle the horse at the withers, clamp himself against its shoulders, grip its sides. Then he'd let the horse carry him along at full tilt. Their bodies would form one, they would have a common soul. He'd whisper in the horse's ear: "You're a thoroughbred and you're brave. Your trot is a dance that comes from the depths of time." The animal would snort, continue its course among its cohorts. "You mustn't go in that direction. You have many valleys still to cross, ice-cold rivers to drink from." He'd pressure its flank. The animal would react to his voice, his movements. "Come, it won't be backing out. You're too proud not to carry this through. Only put it off for a time. Wait until next summer. In the meantime, we'll cross the continent from one end to another." The song of America would speak to the horse's mind. "Don't go with your brothers. You have to see the sun rise again tomorrow. We'll look at landscapes of extraordinary beauty, we'll cleave a passage through the storms." The animal would slow its pace. "Yes, that's it, stay, come with me. On another day we'll go to where your brothers are going." The horse would let the others run past. "It's not time yet for you to disappear." The horse would shake its head and rear, its mane would float in the early morning wind. And while the herd forged ahead into the waves, the horse would turn on itself as though dancing on air, its eyes sparkling, and they'd ride back up the river. "Now we'll save another helpless soul." They would gallop in the wind until they reached Rolder, climb the path to the Hatford house. There, Scott would make the animal rear up. The mustang would let out a long whinny. Mom would appear on the porch. She'd understand right away, slip on her jacket, and come join him. She'd mount like an Amazon. They'd ride past town, across plains and valleys. And the devil himself wouldn't know where to find them.

#

As he walked along Capitol Street, the blast of a car horn startled him from his thoughts. Tim Matthews was driving at walking speed behind him at the wheel of his blue 1957 Chevrolet coupe with its shiny fins and chrome trim, its motor throbbing. Tim was barely 15, he lived in the upper-crust neighborhood of East Rolder, in a three-story house on Jefferson. The Matthews family had made its fortune in the 1920s, before the crash, when Rolder proudly supplied all of the American Southwest with pots and pans, thanks to factories dotting the edges of town on land that belonged to the Matthewses. The warehouses had been abandoned for years, but the Matthewses still lived in style. Since he turned 14, Tim had been seen all over town at the wheel of his father's cars, and the deputy sheriff had never said a word. Sometimes Tim made his engine scream through the streets of Rolder, and sometimes he crossed the town slowly, the top down and the windows open.

Tim Matthews called out to him in a loud and threatening voice. He said that Scott had been seen talking to Jenny Blanchard. He had good information that young Hatford was trying to seduce Ted Harvey's girl. He should be careful. A man's honor was at stake. No one appreciated that kind of behavior around here. No one wanted to see a native of the valley on his way to the front being double-crossed by the son of an outsider, a weakling, a lowlife, the dregs of the county. Tim was telling him as his friend. He wouldn't point the finger at Scott or take part in spreading the rumor. That wasn't his way. He had his pride. But Scott should watch out. Not everyone in Rolder was as easy-going as he. There were people who'd be glad to settle their score with the Hatfords. Tim Matthews beeped his horn once more and sped away with a roar, leaving a thick trail of gray smoke in his wake.

Scott chased Matthews's words from his mind. There were always rumors flying around Rolder. The town bulged with grudges and grievances. Everyone acted as a shadowy witness to his neighbor's doings. Those who'd watched each other grow up were watching each other grow old. The ill fortune that struck your house knocked at every other door as well. Your morning greeting betrayed the fears you'd suffered during the night. Nothing that was said was ever forgotten, nothing that was done ever stayed in the dark. Moments of solemn joy, secret indulgences, all were shared. Nothing hinted at the power, grandeur, grace of the world. A muted hostility clouded every mind. Rolder was a big family. Just not his.

X

He followed Hawthorne Street to Lincoln Avenue, entered Baker's General Store to buy a pack of chewing gum but walked out when he saw the line in front of the cashier. Suddenly, he stopped. His eyes were arrested by a figure on the opposite sidewalk. For a moment he was unsure, but no, it really was him, this man walking in the light of day, his appearance less familiar than usual, the tan-colored fedora he never wore jammed on his head and the light gray suit that lived in his closet drooping from his too-small shoulders and bagging at the hips. Dressed as he was, his father cut an oddly handsome figure. Someone who didn't know him might think he was going to work. Or just coming back from Sunday service. Or out for a business lunch. But what was his father doing at this time of day, all dressed up, walking with a sure step down Lincoln Avenue? Scott hesitated to follow. He would have liked nothing better than to walk through town next to his father. It had never happened. At least, as far back as he could remember. But he had no clue as to what brought his father onto the avenue, dressed as he was. Confused, he preferred to follow at a distance from across the street.

When he reached Bob's Shoes, Jeffrey Hatford stopped and looked to right and left. Did his father have a premonition about something? Or, well—couldn't he dream?—maybe his father was looking for him, there was nothing so unusual about a father going downtown to stroll through the streets with his son, what was so crazy about that? Who has never heard his name called while standing in the midst of a crowd? Yes, his father had come to find him. He'd woken up this morning with the mad idea of spending the late afternoon with his son. He'd worn his only suit for the occasion and his magnificent hat. It was no ordinary day when Jeffrey Hatford decided to go for a walk with his son, and his son would see how elegant he could be, a man like any other and his father to boot. Surely Scott deserved this mark of attention. He was an obedient son, respectful, honest, a good student moreover, even if some odd thoughts had crossed his mind when he picked up that gun, but what adolescent doesn't stray off the path at times, who hasn't at one time or another thought of blasting his father with a lever-action Winchester, you had to keep things in context, let some things go, and hadn't the kid been properly corrected, heavily punished even, he'd never do that again, the boy understood now, let the faults of the past be erased and we'll start on a new basis, I'm going to put on a suit and wear my hat, if there was ever a time to wear it, this is the day.

He'd walked downtown to meet Scott, probably thinking they would see a movie together, something they'd never done, there were good movies playing that he could see with his son, not a war film, the war was over, the horror of it had lasted long enough, times had changed, it had just taken him a while to understand, that's all, but the main point was to come to terms with things, life was one long apprenticeship, and I, Jeffrey Romuald Hatford, have learned from life.

Scott quickened his pace. He'd never imagined that a day would come when, twenty-four hours after holding his mother in his embrace, he would be walking arm-in-arm with his father. Everything around him seemed to grow brighter. The sidewalk sparkled under his feet. A light scent floated on the air. Hope was dawning in Rolder. He wondered what plans his father had made for after the screening. Maybe his father would take him to Taylor's for dinner. They'd share a prime rib of beef and talk about the movie. They'd express a few reservations about the acting but agree that it was a good film. Then his father would ask him how things were going at school, what his favorite subject was, what direction he saw himself taking later. Then they'd walk back across town together, his father's hand slipped into his.

Jeffrey Hatford turned suddenly, looked over at the opposite sidewalk, toward Scott, and held out his arms. He felt his legs tremble. His heart beat like a drum. His father was reaching out to him for a reason other than to give him a hard slap. He tried to contain his joy. Above all, don't lose your head, don't cry victory. This was a first, a new state, a novel inclination, which he had to protect from itself as well as from the outside world. He had to walk forward calmly, not hurry, not alarm his father by showing too much sentiment, not crowd this man whom war had cast adrift, turned indifferent, and who seemed at this moment to have been reawakened to the good in the world. Too sharp an enthusiasm might startle him, spook him, make him run. Jeffrey Hatford's spirit was like a mustang's, mettlesome, untamable, and entrenched behind pride. Today, as if by miracle, the man was lowering his guard, holding his fear in abeyance, taking a giant step, and revisiting the waters where his fellow men came to drink. The Hatfords would henceforth celebrate this day, the day of reconciliation, the day when this man walked on water, rekindled a cold hearth, the Sunday when his father opened his arms to him, they would be talking about it for generations, his children, the children of his children, would observe the date, thank the heavens for having sounded the truce, given their glow to the dark night, yes, after the Day of the Dead, Resurrection Day, and Ash Wednesday, there is now Reconciliation Day, a long Sunday of prayer extolling the Lord, a song of glory to the Almighty, who transforms men, makes them affable and mild, delivers lives trapped in the abyss.

He couldn't contain his joy any longer. He decided to cross the avenue to join his father. He reached the crosswalk. The light turned against him. The waiting cars started up. A slew of vehicles flowed past. When the flow stopped, a woman was snuggling in his father's arms.

He stepped back, as if stunned. He couldn't understand what his eyes had seen. He looked across the road. His father was kissing the woman. No kiss had ever lasted so long, not even in the movies. Maybe it was a movie kiss, something faked? Or maybe the young woman was a distant cousin, met by chance? A long separation deserved a big embrace. Dear cousin, I'd like to introduce you to my son, see how big he's grown, I'm proud of him, the pride of my bloodline, so what do you think, Shirley, will you come with us to see *Spartacus*? The traffic signal turned. His father and the young woman walked along hand in hand. Scott, still on the opposite sidewalk, walked alongside them. He observed his father. His father looked happy, carefree, light-hearted. He'd never seen his father in this mood. The woman clung to his father's side. Her mouth, her eyes were extravagantly painted. She looked like the girl that Mike had introduced him to in the parking lot of a drive-in on the outskirts of Phoenix, a girl who went by the name of Molly and would perform any act for $1.50. This woman wasn't Molly, and his father was a man of the worst kind. His father felt no shame at anything, lied as easily as he breathed, with the same unhinged studiousness that he applied to drinking or to beating a person who defied his will, his father was an abject creature, cruel, savage, and contemptible.

They wouldn't be going to the movies.

Perched on her high heels, the woman stood taller than his father. She wore a dress that was cinched in at the waist, accentuating her hips and breasts, they strolled side by side through the streets of Rolder, his father and that woman, Oh, how their laughter echoed in his ears! She cackled, he belly-laughed. They cracked up constantly, at the slightest comment, what could ever be so funny, these two grotesque characters, you think you're swimming in happiness when you're wallowing in muck, she was tossing her head back, a look of triumph on her face, repairing the disorder to her hairdo with a studied gesture of her hand. They stopped at every moment, like dogs marking their territory, she flung herself at his neck as though to keep him from leaving, and he squeezed her in his arms, his father kept another woman, and at every step a burst of laughter, why was this funny?

He crossed the street to get closer to this seeming happiness. He wasn't afraid that his father would turn around, his father didn't frighten him anymore, this little man at the feet of a tall blonde, Jeffrey in Wonderland. Now he could hear his voice, speaking with an actor's affectation, actors are clowns, the deep voice of a male in rut, you're behaving like an animal, this tender gaze, your heart isn't all dried up, a trifle can make you laugh, you're not the person people think, you've lied up and down the line, you walk arm in arm with a woman, you're capable of gentleness, you're fawning and attentive, a form of ardor animates your face, your whole self is unfamiliar, I don't recognize my father, Lord have pity on me, a miracle, no ball and chain attaches to his leg, his father no longer drags his left foot, or hardly at all, he must be making an extraordinary effort and tormenting his flesh to hide his limp, and when they stop walking, these constant countless kisses, their lips a shoal of little red fish, his father who never gives kisses, never holds out his cheek or brings his lips close, his mouth now swallowed halfway down this woman's throat, have you no shame, acting like this in front of the whole world, every passerby watching you out of the corner of his eye, all of Rolder judging and condemning you, laughing at you harder than you are laughing, and now her voice, pitched high and ringing false, whispering in your ear, murmuring endearments, suddenly vibrant and alive, joyous cries swirling through the air, now they're kissing again, madly, dancing a crazy dance, the street is not a masked ball, and to think that their kisses rise to heaven alongside people's supplications and entreaties, their laughter mixing with our prayers, sullying the place where souls find rest.

His father pulled a pack of cigarettes from his pocket, flicked one out with his index, she took it delicately, carried it between two fingers to her lips, he spun the wheel of his lighter, and while she inhaled, their two faces lit by the flame, they devoured each other with their eyes, his father and the other woman, under his watchful gaze.

They stopped at the entrance to an old hotel with a shabby front. They exchanged a few words on the sidewalk, suddenly unsure at the sight of this miserable inn. And their uncertainty was somehow pitiful. The woman wrapped her arms around Jeffrey Hatford's neck, kicking up a leg behind her like one of those starlets Scott hated, she smoothed the collar of his jacket, took the man by the arm and led him through the door. They walked arm in arm like a bride and groom approaching the altar. Scott watched them horrified, unable to look away, an assiduous witness to abjection, his eyes riveted on the source of his distress, nailed to his fate, helpless in the grip of his suffering, seeking neither support nor reassurance, and nowhere was there a shadow of consolation in the bleak light of the day.

He remained speechless in the midst of the town's noisy bustle, in the awful truth of the moment, obstinately stuck across from the Hotel of Broken Dreams, whose walls dripped grief onto the asphalt pavement. Paralyzed by his inability to do anything, he stayed stuck in place. A sad song rose from his soul, climbed into the air above him, an ode to the splendid vision he'd just had snatched from him, a father's affection, folded into a dark treasure of deeply felt caresses. He waited on the chance of an about-face, sure that his father would think better of it, return to his rightful mind, experience grace, find the exit route, quit this place of affliction and waste so ill-befitting a man.

Scott's eyes were drawn to the hotel's third floor, where a light had gone on. He counted silently, fourth room from the right, gathered his courage and went in. The receptionist stared at him from behind his glasses.

"I need to find my mother and father in room 304."

"You mean, room 314?"

"Right, 314."

"They just went up. Are you sure it's your mother and your father?"

"Who else would it be?"

He climbed the stairs to the third floor, stopped in front of room 314, pressed his ear to the door, heard moaning, then cries, then, more distinctly, the woman shouting: "Hold me tighter!" He decided he'd heard enough, spun on his heels, and headed down the stairs. The receptionist called out: "Leaving already?" He said nothing. He went out on the sidewalk and walked away, then came back and stood in front of the hotel. He would have liked to talk to the woman. He wanted some explanation from his father. I don't expect excuses. I'm not looking for a quarrel, just a word to help me understand what drives you to behave this way, to lie as well as to inflict pain, to spread unhappiness day after day. He paced the sidewalk near the hotel entrance. The shop window on the right was a furniture store whose armchairs and coffee tables were on sale, the purchase of a three-seat leather couch earned you a free coffee table, the purchase of a table earned you a free bedside lamp, and the purchase of a Sealy mattress at $39.95 came with a free bed pillow, please note that prices are valid only through November 2. With one eye on the hotel entrance, he loitered in front of the shop window, whose shelves displayed side by side a bottle of Budweiser beer, a bottle of Carling beer, a bottle of Early Time bourbon, a bottle of Gilbey's gin, several piles of cigarette packs—Pall Mall, Chesterfield, Lucky Strike, Old Gold, L&M, and Newport—a bag of Ken-L Ration dog biscuits, an aerosol can of Old Spice shaving cream, a bottle of Avon scent for men, a bottle of Angel Skin hair tonic, a stack of Campbell's tomato soup cans, a can of Chef Boyar-dee spaghetti and meatballs, a can of Star-Kist tunafish, a box of Oreo cookies, a box of Magic Crystals powdered milk, a big can of A&P coffee, a packet of mentholated mints, a box of Bayer aspirin, a box of Alka Seltzer, a Sunbeam Rollmaster safety razor, a package of New and Young girdles from Warner's, and a copy of *Life* magazine from January 13, 1961 with Clark Gable on the cover.

High heels clicked across the pavement. The girl was coming out of the hotel. She walked alone, her dress creased, her hair disheveled, her face caked with make-up. He thought of his mother's beauty. He fell in behind her. At the crosswalk he stopped next to her and said, "I'm the son of Jeffrey and Meredith Hatford."

The girl burst out laughing. "And I'm the queen of England!" The light turned. She crossed the street. "Yup, the queen of England!" And her horrible laugh rang through the air.

He walked back the way he'd come. He saw his father come out of the hotel. He hesitated to approach him. He watched the man walk slowly along Lincoln Avenue, his hat in his hand, a smug look on his face. He'd seen enough.

#

God of a dark world, why was I treated to that sight? Why am I being punished? What have I done that I should be a witness to my father's crime? Lord, when I next see my mother, help me to hold back my tears, strengthen my weakness. May I be struck dumb if I am tempted to reveal this ugly transgression. May there be in my eyes no admission of any kind, may my memories remain hidden from her sight, though she sees through me, guesses at what troubles me. May I reveal nothing of all that I have seen. Although I have promised never to lie, Mom's sorrow goes beyond vows and is above laws. My mother's heart is a sanctuary, fragile, pure, and delicate. Allow me to keep my suffering quiet and my lips shut. But Lord, You who are just, don't let this act go unpunished. Give my father the fate reserved for those who defy You. Don't forgive this man who offends You by day and curses You by night, this man who, each day, trashes everything a son dreams of.

He turned onto Capitol Street, walking first one way then the other, decided to go as far as Duby's, looked through the plate-glass window for Jenny, found her behind the counter, her back to the window, went into the empty restaurant, sat down at a table.

"You're back," she said, "and this time it'll be my treat, you don't talk much when you have that sad look, and you don't look like Elvis at all, you're the spitting image of your mother, she's beautiful, I can understand why you're not interested in girls yet, her so magnificent, the image of loveliness, other girls just don't make the grade, and such a well of tenderness in her deep eyes, it isn't going to be easy to find a treasure like that among the other girls, chances are you'll be disappointed, spend your life waiting, the ladies will have to hang on tight; because the love of others, that's something you'll get in spades, and I know something about it, I love a lot, not everyone, luckily, but a lot, I don't measure the love I give, I give without counting, it gives me pleasure, but sure, there's no point in resenting your mother, she's preparing the ground for us, she's cutting the trail, she's planting the seed for the great emotions, so, sure, afterwards our heartthrobs are going to seem silly to you, women's hearts are going to seem limited when you've known such an expanse of love, we're going to seem narrow in our bodices and our skirts, with our little problems, our little quirks, in the end I'm not so sure your mother is doing you a favor, loving you as she does, but too much love is probably better than not enough, look what happens when you don't get your share, you're always looking for it, you give yourself to someone the moment he shows an interest in you, offers the slightest comfort, and since no one kept a loving watch over my crib, of course, if anyone sends even a glance my way it puts me in a tailspin, even if the glance is slightly oblique, aimed more at my cleavage than my soul, I don't have any illusions, you know, my soul means nothing to anyone, Ted doesn't even know that I have one, someone else might fall into despair but the good Lord gave me a happy disposition, because life is nicely balanced, and if you can't have everything, you also can't have nothing at all, I inherited my disposition from my mother, she has an even temper too, it makes a difference in my line of work, people don't want to come in here and find you apples one day and oranges the next, they want you to smile at them, and that makes sense, it isn't the quality of Walter Duby's meat that brings them back a second time, they like it when we talk to them, take an interest in them, which works out well for me since I take an interest in men, I mean mankind generally, you knew that, you're not the type to take everything at face value, but you want to be careful all the same not to get stuck in the abstract, people who live in the abstract lose their sense of reality, they don't fully enjoy anything, they go out at noon expecting nightfall, you've got to keep it simple, noon is noon, the hour when customers start showing up, OK I'm not going to start talking shop with you, I don't see you ending up behind the counter of a coffee shop anyway, that's another thing a person can tell, with your big forehead, with what's shining at the back of your eyes and looks a lot like intelligence, even if what I'm seeing this afternoon is all sadness, and I'm no Einstein but I have a good idea of why you're sad, because from my counter I see what's happening on the sidewalk and the street, not always the brightest picture, and what the adults in your life served up today, you're going to say it's none of my business, but when it comes to your father, I'd rather see him drunk at the bar than in the arms of some girl out of nowhere, although, that girl isn't exactly unknown in the neighborhood, the opposite really, and I don't want to make you any more miserable since you're on the verge of tears already and if there's one thing that gives me the willies it's seeing a man cry, men shouldn't cry, of course, you're not a man yet but you're on the road to being one, you're finding out just what they're capable of, not very pretty, and I'm not just talking about your father, you know, my father was no better, I'm not just saying that to buck you up, it's the truth, my father did his dirty stuff at home, I'd have preferred if he'd done his dirty stuff in broad daylight like your father, having other people see him would have slowed him down, and it would have spared us a lot, my sister and me, but you don't get to choose your son-of-a-bitch of a father, yours could obviously be a bit more discreet, especially when it comes to Anita, and now that I know your mother, I wonder what he sees in that girl, given the rates she charges, but people do what they want with their money, everyone is accountable to the Lord, even if your father and mine think they'll never have to answer for their acts, in spite of what my mother says, that you should never complain, that sorrow comes to each in different forms, that she never even had a father, so which is better? Hey, finish your lemonade and go home, you're starting to weigh me down with your grief."

#

As night fell, the streets grew deserted. The townspeople seemed to be holed up at home. Was it possible that war had been declared and the nuclear alert sounded? Could they be living the world's last hours? He wouldn't have to lie to his mother. He wouldn't have to look into his father's eyes. He set himself little challenges. If he reached the crosswalk before the light changed, his father wouldn't come home again. If he could hold his breath until the door of 58 Roosevelt Street, his father wouldn't come home again. If he reached the edge of the sidewalk at the far end of the street on his left foot, his father wouldn't come home again. A woman emerged from her house with a dog on a leash. A bark echoed through the quiet street. The woman's face showed not the slightest anxiety. The war wouldn't be for tonight.

He made his way like a sleepwalker under the bleak sky. He was ashamed of what he'd seen and of who he was. Passing his old school at 39 Virginia Street, a memory entered his head. He was ten years old. He was coming out of the building with a classmate, Jimmy Lloyd, no Boyd. Jimmy invited him to come over after school. He lived on Jefferson Street at Adview Road. Jimmy's mother shut the door of her Chrysler Newport convertible and came toward them. Say you'll come, we'll go for a swim in the pool! At the same moment, he saw his father a few yards behind, dragging his left leg along the sidewalk, scraping the dirt and raising little clouds of dust. His trousers had slid down around his backside. He was wearing the checked shirt that he always wore and that stank of sweat. He was breathing with a hoarse, rasping sound. About a dozen mothers were standing on the school steps. Jeffrey Hatford passed them and came toward him. Scott was sure that each of the mothers was eyeing his father, noticing his leg, smelling his body odor. He thought he heard scornful laughs. His father had never come to pick him up before. Jimmy's mother took her son's schoolbag. The boy said, I've asked Scott to come for a visit. Oh, what a nice idea! His father reached them. I can't, I'm so sorry, I have to get home. That's all right, Scott, said Jimmy's mother, stroking her son's neck, we'll do it another time. He remembered his feeling of shame when his father came to stand between him and Jimmy, facing the woman, and the glance of disappointment his father shot him when the mother and son held their silence for a moment, waiting for Scott to introduce the man next to him. But he hadn't said a word. He was afraid that if he lingered, Jimmy's mother would become aware of his father's smell, catch sight of his dirt-flecked shoes. Up to that point, he'd had no father, as far as his classmates knew, only an appealing and lovely mother, delicately scented, who handed around greetings to the teachers and the other mothers, and offered Jimmy Boyd Holloway All-Day Suckers.

Today, it was his father's turn to avoid him on the sidewalk.

He felt implicated in Jeffrey Hatford's crime. Then he reasoned with himself. Did his father think of Jimmy Boyd when he embraced the whore of Rolder? Did he hear Jimmy Boyd's voice when the whore of Rolder sighed in his ear?

He headed up the dirt road he lived on, his unnamed Blank Street, passed Los Lobos, which was quiet in the gathering dark. He walked slowly, arduously, his strength all gone, emptied of rebellion and rage, his mind filled with sadness and dark thoughts, from which emerged the indomitable image of his father, his gawky gait, his sorrowful eyes, his gray face, his mouth set in a grim line. He reached the fence, crossed the porch, entered, found the house empty, made his way to his room, collapsed on the bed, burst into tears, cried in the vast depth of the night, with all the accumulated sadness of his heart. Between the walls, there at the top of the hill, no sound was heard other than his crying, his unleashed distress. Lord, is a man who cheats on his wife under his son's eyes worthy of being called a man?

He got up, went into the living room, sat on the sofa in the place normally reserved for his father—whoever sat there courted a major fit of anger. He pretended to reach for a can of beer and said, in the deepest voice he could muster: "I'm going to rot in hell!" He sat there a few moments longer, his eyes fixed on the dark television screen, then rose to fetch himself a glass of water. At that moment he heard the slow scraping of his father's footsteps outside the door. He rushed into his room.

A sliver of light showed at the crack in the door. The man's footsteps sounded on the floor. The door opened. His father poked his head into the room, stared at him coldly, and withdrew. He hadn't hoped for this calm, but in the great well of silence, he found something disturbing. The walls hadn't trembled, no swear words had been spoken. He didn't know if he should be relieved or saddened. Would he have preferred, in place of this impassive mask, a torrent of rage? Had he wanted to confront his father's anger? He felt capable of it. His father, for all his guilt, forbade any rebellion, condemned him to impotence as well as sorrow, took from him what might have made him a man. His father had come to taunt him, take even his anger away, add contempt to infamy. His father's cruelty knew no limits. The sound of the television drifted to him. His father was watching the news. They were talking about war. Scott listened. The situation had escalated significantly. A U.S. Air Force plane, flying over Cuba, had been shot down by a surface-to-air missile. The pilot, Major Rudolf Anderson, was dead. This was the same man who had taken the first photographs of the nuclear missile facilities, the hero of the hour. Commentators were arguing about how best to respond. Most wanted to strike back quickly and definitively. Carpet-bomb the Soviet missile silos. Invade Cuba with the half-million Marines already on a war footing. Send bombers into Cuban airspace. The blockade ordered by President Kennedy was inadequate and would have no effect. The United States had been humiliated more than enough. The country's honor was at stake, as well as its survival. Cuba should be flattened by bombs, the Soviet ships should be sunk and the submarines accompanying them hunted down. One of their correspondents then summed up the situation. If Havana was attacked, the Russians would bomb Berlin. If Berlin was leveled, NATO would fire missiles at Moscow. The Russians would respond with a nuclear strike against Washington. At that point, American nuclear superiority would kick in, and Russia would be obliterated from the map.

There was the sound of a key in the door, the squeak of hinges, and heels across the floor. A moment later, he heard his mother's voice.

"You're back?"

"What, I'm not allowed?"

"Sure, of course."

"Then why so surprised?"

She hadn't expected to see him.

"And why are you home at this time of night?"

Gladys Chapman was back from sick leave and had offered to take her shift.

"Are you sure that's really the reason?"

She wasn't aware of any other.

"There's one I can think of. You've come to see if I'm here. You're spying on me, aren't you?"

She wasn't spying on him.

"Oh, right. You've ordered your son to do it for you."

Her son had other things to do than spy on him.

"Then why was he following me all over town?"

He hadn't been following him at all.

"I saw him peering at me in the street earlier on. Are you going to keep having me followed and made to look like a bastard in the eyes of my son?"

"Your son doesn't need my help for that."

"Just what are you saying?"

She wasn't saying anything.

"Don't push me too far."

"I'm not pushing you."

"You know, I could push you too, if I felt like it."

She knew that.

"I've never lifted my hand against you, never struck a woman. So don't provoke me!"

She wasn't provoking him.

"What else have you been doing since you walked in?"

"I'm looking for a place to sit."

"You're provoking me. Even though you know it doesn't take much to push me over the edge."

She was aware of that.

"Don't go dogging me. I've had it with you dogging me. No one's ever dogged me the way you do. You hound me, spy on me, persecute me. You make me look like a son of a bitch in front of my boy. You take me for a failure. That's how you see me, isn't it, the two of you, as a dimwitted son of a bitch? Why don't you have the guts to tell me that? You always get to wear the white hat. And when you've pushed me as far as I can go, when I can't control myself anymore, you'll play the victim, because you know I can't control myself, I haven't got your strength, I haven't been educated to control my emotions, you goddamn slut!"

"I forbid you to call me names."

"And who are you to forbid me anything in my own home? I can say whatever comes into my head. Meredith Hatford is a goddamn slut, a whore who sleeps with doctors."

She shouted for him to stop.

"I can sing it if I want."

"Stop!"

"Are you threatening to hit me? No one threatens Jeffrey
Hatford. You know that, right? I've got gallons of blood on my
hands, as if you didn't know. Do you think I've forgotten how to
fight, just because I've got a bad leg? Is it war you want? All right,
take that, you little saint! And that! Oh, we're not so high and
mighty now that we're lying on the floor. Not so easy to look
down on me, is it? And now you're going to beg. Beg! That's a
direct order from Lieutenant Hatford! Entreat your husband the
way you entreat your stinking God. I could crush your pretty little
face under my boots. Nobody would recognize you at that hospital
of yours. Even that slime-ball Doctor Jenkins wouldn't want you
anymore. Beg your husband's forgiveness."

She asked for forgiveness.

"Forgive me, who?"

"Forgive me, Jeffrey."

"Forgive me, Lieutenant Hatford! You won't do it again?"

She said no.

"No, who?"

"No, Lieutenant Hatford."

"You won't have me followed?"

"No, Lieutenant Hatford."

"You won't make me lie anymore?"

"No, Lieutenant Hatford."

"You won't make me strike a woman again?"

"No, Lieutenant Hatford."

"Go on, get up. You're not all that bad, really."

XI

He climbs into the car, whose engine is already running. He's being told to hurry. His stomach rumbles with hunger. He's wearing yesterday's clothes over his pyjamas. He was woken up before dawn. His mother shook him by the shoulders. There was something dark in her eyes. He swung his feet to the ground. The floor was freezing. She threw his clothes at him from the door. He hadn't taken off his pyjamas. By the time he realized it, she was already going down the front steps. Now that he's sitting in the back seat of the car, he puts it all together. They are running away from Rolder.

The car roars off. The tires crunch on the gravel. They drive down the dirt track. They take the curves too fast, brush against tree branches, shave the fronts of houses. They get to the lower town.

The facades are steeped in half-light. Here and there, a window lights up. They take Hawthorn Street, then Roosevelt, drive through a red light at the crossroads of Lincoln Avenue. They barrel at a fast clip through the valley.

"Lie down, get a little more sleep," says Mom.

"But what if Dad wakes up?"

"Dad is not going to wake up."

"Are you saying . . . you killed Dad?"

"Your dad has a full day of sleep ahead of him."

"You drugged him!"

"Let's just say that his final whiskey last night must have had a little aftertaste."

"Are you allowed to do that?"

"No, sweetheart, we're going to Hell. And the worst of it is that we'll see your father there! Go to sleep now."

He stretches out on the back seat. He worries that if he closes his eyes, he'll wake up in the flames of Hell. He fights briefly. He tumbles into a deep sleep.

He is walking along the Grand Canyon, looking down on the glittering Colorado River swathed in pure and absolute silence. He grows dizzy, loses his balance, falls into the void. He wakes up from his nightmare in a sweat. A rainstorm is battering the car— autumn's sudden fury.

His mother's expression in the rearview mirror is one of recovered calm. She catches his glance and smiles at him. She reaches into her purse on the passenger seat and passes back to him a pack of cookies. He devours the sweet cakes and, with his mouth full, asks if they've been driving a long time. More than two hours, she answers. He realizes that he's missed a morning at school. He'll never know his grade on the math test. He thought he got all right answers. An unexplained absence could get him expelled. Would he need a note from his father?

A highway sign announces "Flagstaff 32 miles." Mom is humming "Love Me Tender."

He is in no mood to sing. He doesn't like this road. He hates the fall rains. He's not happy about the direction things are taking. He would prefer to turn around and go home.

Soon his father will wake up, fly into a rage, break everything he can get his hands on, fetch the ax from the yard, demolish the dining-room table, attack the sideboard, break down the doors. Then he will set fire to the house. His room will be reduced to ashes. He'll be kicked out of school. He won't hang around with

Mike anymore. He won't be able to roam the streets of Rolder. He'll never see Mr. Brown or Jenny again, never hear Pastor Simpson preach, he won't take off running every weekday down the highway, he'll never climb the hill again. He'll stop having a father.

His life was taking a turn toward the unknown. He's more afraid of the unknown than he is of his father. His father is predictable, his fits of anger are expected. He knows his father's favorite swear words by heart. He's gotten used to the blows. He knows to the split second when his father's fury will erupt. He can read his father's mind like an open book. What does the unknown have in store for us?

His mother promises that they'll stop at the next gas station. They pass three of them without slowing down. He ignores his hunger.

They finally stop at a roadside diner made to look like a Wild West saloon. He orders a steak, roasted potatoes, and some doughnuts. She chooses the tuna salad. She says she wants to get past Flagstaff. And after Flagstaff? She mentions Denver. Wouldn't he like to visit Denver? She has an old friend who lives there. He says nothing. He's never thought of going to Denver. He doesn't know a thing about Denver. She looks right at him and asks if he's angry that she's taken him down this path. How could he be angry at his mother? He barely manages to loathe his father. He feels incapable of resentment. Hate just isn't in his make-up.

Would he have preferred to stay home? No, he lies. It was the first time his father had ever struck her. What would come next, a rifle bullet? He says she made the right decision. Tears run silently down his mother's face. Immediately, he starts to cry.

They get back on the road. The storm has passed. The sky is clear and intensely blue, a miracle of light. In the distance, at the foot of the high-piled rock, stand tall monoliths. He remembers that Geronimo once trained his warriors on this land. In places, the peaks join to form granite arches in the air. Everything rises up, like a prayer that Earth might make to Heaven.

They flee through these immensities. His father often said that there was nowhere, not a place on earth, where they would be safe from him. Not in the chasms of the canyons, not on the tops of *mesas* would they be sheltered from his wrath. The whole earth would not be vast enough for them. He would catch them at the far edge of the world. Let them run away! Lieutenant Hatford had had to deal with tougher customers than they. In Korea, in the muddy expanses of the rice fields, his division had been destroyed. But not him. Thousands of veterans of World War II, who'd defeated the great German army, had fallen to the attacks of the Chinese. But not him. His own brother had died during the taking of Seoul. His younger brother was killed, but death had left him alone. Three hundred thousand soldiers in the Allied forces had met their death. But he had survived. He kept it all in his memory. He remembered everything. The terror of the G.I.'s inside the dark forests, with the Chinese hiding behind every tree, thousands of

Chinese in every wood, attacking night and day. Under torrential rains, in torrid heat, in the Cheorwon Valley, on every hill, taken and lost again, trench warfare. The Chinese tanks had charged toward them at Pusan, and they had to hold the line no matter what, MacArthur had told them that, then General Walker, then Lieutenant General Ridgway after Walker died riding in his jeep. The Chinese forces attacked in waves, bearing down on every position—hold your positions!—crossed the Nakdong River, and Pusan, a living hell, crumbled under a hail of bombs. The small-arms combat in the Punchbowl, where munitions ran short, the men he had stabbed with his bayonet, yes, with his bayonet, eleven single- handedly, blood had spurted from their bodies, his hands bathed in gore. And did they know where he got the strength to hold out in the mud fields, surrounded by corpses? What force had allowed him to sink his blade into the guts of his enemies? What miracle had helped him avoid the bullets when the men around him were falling like flies? The thought of seeing them again. The prospect that he would once more be with his son. Just let them try to get away from him! Arizona wasn't big enough. The United States wasn't big enough. He would catch them on the Brooklyn Bridge, in the wilds of Montana. The American continent was too small for the three of them. Let them cross the sea and ask Castro for asylum! He'd find them in any dive in Havana. He wasn't afraid of the Reds. He'd killed Browns, he'd killed Yellows, he would obliterate the Reds. That's the way Jeffrey Hatford talked.

Three times they'd tried to run away from Rolder already, and each time their escape had ended in failure. The first time he knew only through his mother's stories. He'd been three years old. She had put him in the back of an old Ford that her friend Linda Harvey had lent to her—a rust bucket, a wreck. Mom had made a stop at the gas station in the middle of Rolder. She'd begged the pump jockey to hurry. No need to fill the tank all the way. Here, take these two dollars, thanks. As she held out the money, she saw Jeffrey Hatford's blue 1947 Chevrolet nosing toward them, driving unhurriedly, its headlights on in broad daylight. The car had driven slowly past the gas station without stopping. When Mom turned the key in the ignition, there was no sound from the engine. She turned the key again. The car remained silent. There was a squeal of tires at the far end of the street. A few seconds later, the Chevy had rolled up to block their passage. They were driven back to the solitary hill.

He remembered bits and pieces of the second attempt. It had occurred three years earlier. They were in a 1952 Oldsmobile that ran perfectly. He'd never known how his mother got hold of it. They'd made it past Phoenix and were headed toward Tucson. His mother had never driven so fast, that he could remember. She was constantly checking the rearview mirror. A few miles from Tucson, a car on their right started honking at them. From the back seat, Scott sang out, "Look, Mom, Dad is passing us!" They had turned and gone home.

He remembered every second of the last attempt, which had happened two years earlier. They were in the 1957 Cadillac Coupe de Ville, whose keys Mom had lifted from Dad while he was sleeping. The Cadillac ran well. But the passenger-side window didn't close all the way and let in air. He remembered the cold wind. They'd gotten as far as Belen. As they crossed the line into New Mexico, Mom had said, "We're safe!" They had stopped in a motel along Route 60, near Magdalena. They were assigned a room in the wing of the building that gave onto the parking lot. Mom parked in front of the door and carried the suitcases in. They'd slept in the same bed—the biggest bed he'd ever seen. In the middle of the night, there was a loud knocking at the door. A few seconds later, the door was kicked in. His father loomed over them. His eyes were crazed. Out of his mouth came a stream of insults. His hands swept the air in front of him. Scott had hidden at the far end of the room, crouching behind an armchair. His mother had stood between them facing his father. A man showed up, asked what all the noise was about. His father had rushed at the man, knocked him flat, and returned. He'd pushed Mom aside with a firm sweep of his arm, walked toward his son, grabbed the chair behind which he was crouching, and flung it at the window, which shattered to bits. He'd picked up his son, gently, it has to be said, crossed the room, opened the door of his car, laid him on the back seat, slid behind the wheel, and turned the key in the ignition. They drove back to Rolder. How had he found them? The mystery of it terrified him to this day.

The road is now running along the foot of sandstone cliffs, peaks forming an escort that surrounds and protects them. Above this seamless rampart, the sun is radiant, the air clear. Mesquite bushes, clusters of box elder rise from the ground. Big cars pass them from time to time, old Chevies and Plymouths, brightly colored, with dented doors and full of passengers. They parallel a dry riverbed. Following the river's course, he sees a few stone ruins, the remains of a time when the Anasazi tamed the earth, built hanging gardens. The lava spires, the succession of peaks carved out of rock, form groups of giants rising on the horizon. He tells himself that the soul of the Indian warriors has petrified here. Their spirit reigns over this locality, gives off strength and courage, which he can draw on.

The strain of the trip starts to weigh on him. He looks out at the landscape of sheer cliffs with maple forests at their feet. Soon, not far off, in the Sonoran Desert, the December rains will make lupines and poppies grow by the millions. Maybe some day he will return to visit this area with his mother. Since unhappiness is now behind them.

Passing through a small town, they stop at an eatery, order a coffee for her, an ice cream for him. A man walks over to the jukebox. A few seconds later, the first strains of "Come Fly With Me" fill the room.

"Why are you looking at me that way?" asks Mom.

He says nothing.

"You think it's our song, don't you, your father's and mine? Nothing could be sillier than that story about our song. Anyway, there was no music when your father and I met. You know perfectly well how it happened."

A woman enters, asks in a loud voice whether there is any flour left. Someone tells her that it's a restaurant, not a grocery. The woman explodes with anger. "Today, the only things we need are flour, soldiers, and the protection of our Lord!" Then she turns and marches out.

"There were no violins the day we met", says Mom. "But there was a great deal of kindness in your father's eyes. Under his swagger, there was a real humanity."

"Are we talking about the same man?"

"You're talking about a man who has returned from war. I'm talking about a man setting out for one."

"All men go to war."

"And many don't come back."

"He came back."

"Not really."

"What about us, will we come back?"

She won't come back. Their old life, she explains, belongs to the past. She won't return to it. She'll never see this man again. She won't face his accusatory stare. She won't suffer his anger. She won't lift him again out of the hole he is sinking into. Soon, Jeffrey Hatford will be nothing more to her than the father of her son.

"But for you, it's different. Whether you like it or not, he'll still be your father."

"A brute of a father."

She has explained it to him already, his father was not a brute when they met. Was it the war that changed him, taught him to resort to violence? Was he craftier than the others? Was that why he survived? His brother, Richard, sweet as a lamb, died in Seoul. Might not his father's brutality be a scar he carried from the war?

"Do you want to see the marks of his belt on my backside?"

"I'm giving you clues for when you come back."

"I won't come back!"

His father had learned to kill. He'd been initiated into the religion of war. Thou shalt kill. Thou shalt steal. Thou shalt rape. How do you return to reason once you've come back from a war?

There is a question Scott is dying to ask: "Does war also drive you toward the whores in Rolder?" But he bites his tongue.

"One day, you'll have to forgive your father. Don't worry, though, you have plenty of time ahead of you."

They get back on the road. He sits in the front seat, wants to be beside his mother. As darkness falls, the plateaus, the valleys, absorb the deepening grays. Everything takes on a leaden weariness. They drive east, into dark night. The headlights of the oncoming cars blind them. From time to time, she reaches for his hand and squeezes it. The telephone poles, the houses along the road flit past like ghosts. A giant shadow lies across the earth. He remembers hearing Pastor Simpson talk about the Judgment Day. Has that day come?

"Mom, I'd like to go to sleep for a bit. Can I climb into the back seat?" says Scott.

"Darling, we'll stop in less than an hour. I'd rather have you stay next to me. I don't like driving at night. My eyes can't take the strain. Do you mind staying next to me a while longer?"

He nods.

"Will you always stay next to me?"

He says he will.

They drive alone, going nowhere. His mother stares at the road ahead. She looks unbearably sad. He feels accountable for her sadness. He thinks: Tomorrow, I will provide you rescuing arms, I'll lead you to safety beyond the mountains, just as you once carried me sleeping in my basket. I know now what struggle I'll devote my days to. A son's task is to bring first truths back into being. I'll be the one who walks ahead of you, stays with you, chases your sorrow away, eases your pain. You've put strange ideas in my head. You've taught me to challenge fate, to put my hopes before my fears. I'll walk with dignity, I'll measure up to your standards. The time is past, mother, when we would set off each day to gather the fruits of sorrow and a harvest of misery. Those days are behind us, they're streaming past along the road edge. You're making me a man. Who could I ever be afraid of, what fear could ever touch me?

He wants to cheer his mother up. He knows the way to do it. He says:

"I think I've found what I want to do when I grow up."

"What will you give me if I guess right?"

"Guess away, you'll find out."

"You could be . . . an actor!"

He doesn't want to be an actor. Actors are clowns, actors grow old faster than others, actors go bad from slipping into the skins of random people, from having to learn random stuff. Actors don't have souls of their own.

"OK, you're going to play professional ball with the Mets. Your coach told me you're an excellent pitcher."

His coach flattered her so she'd come watch him play again. He'd noticed the man's behavior, the way he inspected her as soon as her back was turned. He didn't like the way he looked at her, the lecherous glimmer in the man's eyes. More generally, he hated the way men looked at his mother.

"Your father has passed something on to you anyway. So, what do you want to be?"

"I want to be . . . the opposite of my father."

"You are the opposite of your father. You're sweet, you're good. You're my little angel. Tell me what you want to do in life!"

He makes her promise not to laugh, then he says:

"You remember the president's speech in Houston last December ". . . "We choose to go to the moon in this decade, not because it is easy . . ."

". . . but because it is hard, because that challenge is one that we intend to win, and the others too . "

. . ."Where are you going with this?"

"I'd like to be . . . that first man the president was talking about."

"The first . . . to . . . walk . . . on the moon?"

"Am I not as good as anyone else?"

"You're the jewel in America's crown. You'll be the first man to walk on the moon! I'll be there to welcome you back to earth. I'll give you a big kiss before President Kennedy even has time to shake your hand."

He makes her promise not to repeat what he has said to anyone.

"Not to anyone, she says. Not a word until your photograph is on the cover of *Time* magazine."

They drive along the fence line of a military base. At a nearby bus station, several soldiers are hitchhiking. He looks at their uniforms, their jovial expressions, sees pride in their faces, fierce loyalty. What will become of these men?

It's raining again. Out there, a landscape of mountains and bare hills scrolls past, with large clouds in the distance letting loose their showers. Torrents of water pummel the roof of the car. Bursts of rain lash the pavement. Gusts of wind blow bushes sideways across the road. Clouds release their floodgates overhead. The horizon turns black.

Mom drives with her hands clenched on the steering wheel. Her face is tense, her eyes squint ahead. When a car comes toward them, the shards of light cast worrying shadows on her forehead. Her tired features harden in the glare of the headlights. The storm grows more and more violent. Purple flashes zigzag across the sky. Thunder crashes. The heavy downpour makes a continual racket against the roof of the car.

In the distance, suddenly, Scott sees the halos of four headlights. The beams occupy the full width of the road. At first, Scott can't understand how a vehicle can take up so much space, as wide as the road. But as they draw closer, it's clear that two vehicles are heading straight for them. A car is passing a truck.

His mother utters a piercing scream of terror. Scott sees the fright in her face. A terrible sound of metallic fury fills the air. The earth starts to spin. Everything is astonishing and terrible at once, happening at a crazy speed. The moment seems to defy all the laws, the laws of physics and laws of mechanics, the laws of logic and the laws of balance, the laws of gravity and the laws of attraction, the laws of the mind and the laws of ethics, the law of man and the law of God, natural law and God's justice, the law of Moses and the law of the prophets, the law of fate and the law of providence, the laws of the universe and the law of life.

"Lord, Lord," says Mom.

She turns her face toward Scott. She stares at him intensely, avidly, as though to carry away with this one last look all the splendor of her son, to see in this last second an entire existence. She smiles, her face suddenly calm and full of sweetness. An expression of infinite tenderness shines in the depths of her eyes, joy flashing in adversity, radiant beauty refusing to give her son a mask of horror as his last memory.

Night falls on them.

XII

Night is everywhere, wherever he casts his eyes, from earth to sky, on the flanks of the mountains and in the depths of himself, he pushes forward into this dark night, without beginning or end, wherever his steps lead him, his eyes lowered in shame or raised to the heavens, the same deep darkness, he walks without understanding, nothing seems real or beautiful or tranquil, the world has disappeared or it's not the world, the truth and splendor of the world, it's the arrested world, wrapped in silence, frozen and still, the world where nothing changes, stagnant water in a pond that no rain strikes and that nothing ripples, the source of the great silence, an expanse of horror, the other side of the world, to which there is no reason to go and from which it's best to flee, but flight is impossible, terror guides his steps, he is as if carried, he would like to defend himself, or have someone guide him, in this nether world, that a light might shine on what is happening, on what has happened and what will happen and illuminate the night, separate the true from the false, and nothingness from daylight, hold out a hand to him, a familiar voice that would advise him what to do and where to go, because he feels lost, has lost his way and lost his voice, his sense of touch, his sense of smell, all that makes a man, he's trying to find his way, without anyone's steadying arm, with no one to lead and no one to embrace, in this vast desert bigger than the desert, he knows deserts, their long, bluish shadows, and their veil of mist, this is not heaven, and though he normally wonders about everything, is curious about the slightest thing, is eager to know everything, the end and the means, how the sea is blue, not brown or orange, and why the earth turns, he prefers to know nothing about this place he is wandering in, nor why or how he comes to be there, what fate the lands he is entering hold for him, what he sees is enough, ignorance is precious, an asset in this world where nothing is revealed, he doesn't want to know because, he's certain, nothing will lighten his sorrow, his boundless sorrow, will soften the hurt he feels, calm his fear, for his fear is vast, vaster than the desert, he is afraid of the place he has left and the place he is going to, he is afraid of forgetting and afraid of his memory, he dreads the cold that is falling slowly, all around him, the cold that chills the air and chills his mind, a sepulchral cold that numbs his fingers, his toes, his calves, his whole body, and he also dreads no longer feeling the cold, he fears that he will lose his fingers, he gathers around him all the fears of the day, he is afraid of his shadow, he trembles as he breathes, he fears to learn what the night is hiding, the why of this day, he prefers that a veil should cover the darkness, he takes delight in the belief that nothing lasts, hopes it's the case, here, that everything passes, as it does everywhere else, in the known world, the familiar universe, where unending suffering is not known, nor infinite pain, but he suspects that something has happened, something strange, terrible, dire and fatal, something that his age prevents him from understanding, or approaching from afar, or looking at straight on, a heavy premonition crazes his thoughts and numbs his thighs, robs his throat of its ability to make sound: he knows he comes from a place that has gone dark.

Normally his legs would allow him to sprint away, flee this world, this horrible valley, run beside the big desert, cross the mountains, leave this accursed place, rejoin the other world where stars lie sleeping, he can't feel his legs, his body doesn't respond, any more than his mind staves off his fears or the dark suspicions that inhabit his soul and speak a cruel language to his thoughts, one he doesn't want to hear and doesn't understand, he would like to know what he is walking toward, see a pale light in the dim distance shrouded in pain, shrouded in twilight, hear a voice murmur in the wind, a familiar voice, but no tree rustles under the wind's push, in this place where he's walking, time is not passing, time is suspended from his unmoving lips, everything has stopped beating, the minutes and the hours, the hearts and the hands, it's the cold eternal night of naked souls in the horrible valley, into whose depths, on this day, at this hour, he has dropped as one drops from the sky.

And long after he first sank into the night, into the dark and heavy air where all voices are silent, where nothing has an odor, a color, a shadow, he believes he sees in the distance a hint of light, a pale glint in the absolute dark, yes, something in the depths of the shadows starts to shine, a droplet of honey in a brackish ocean, stars, he doubts it, he hasn't the heart to look at stars, his heart laid low by the horrible mystery before him, unfairly cruel, savage, and implacable, can it be that from the weariness of this long walk, which no extended hand, no other comfort relieves, that from this endless wandering in a dark city his damaged mind, his staring eyes see quarters of the moon shimmering where the sky is bare, empty of all hope, freighted with misery, but that's not it, the light becomes more defined as he approaches it, a wavering glow, elusive but now no longer trembling, a fixed point in his restless wandering, the glow accompanies him, as the sparkling of waves follows you along the shoreline, and when he stops, the light holds still and when he starts up again, it escorts him again, a gift from above, the glow comes near, takes a corner of the darkness and overwhelms it, lighting the road by its simple presence, he confronts this strange glow head-on, and understands its nature, why it's there and what it expresses, this familiar brightness has lit up all the mornings in the world, and now sends its light over the ruins of the day, it's the shine of his mother's glance just above him, her beautiful expressive eyes looking at him, watching over his progress, sparks of splendor, lightness, joy, a wave of heat that manages to melt terror, eclipse the dark, breathe sweetness into the chill wind of night.

XIII

He emerged from sleep slowly. He had no idea what time it was. He couldn't really remember what had happened the day before. What exactly had happened? Recollection came in snatches. Unknown landscapes filed past. Rain was falling. Mom smiled at the wheel of a car. The rest was confused, wrapped in mystery. He stopped searching his memory. The warm sheets reassured him. He was returning from a dark world. Nothing now threatened him. Time and space seemed powerfully arrested. And the immobility that he'd once dreaded now appealed to him. The storm had passed.

He felt a hand stroking his forehead, sensed someone speaking softly in his ear. He recognized the sound of his father's voice, but his kindness of expression and gentleness of tone were at odds with the way he usually spoke. The whispering continued. He had to acknowledge that it really was his father. He inferred that it was his father's hand on his face. His father was beside him and wasn't scolding him, dragging him out of bed, slapping him, insulting him, yelling, he was staying calm and attentive. Times had changed.

A tube inserted down his throat pumped air into his lungs. Nourishing liquids entered his body through his veins. Strong hands gripped him by the shoulders and the hips, turned him over, scrubbed his skin, cleaned him. Things were done without his intervention.

His legs didn't respond. His ribs oppressed him. His back felt as though compacted, his nose, his left shoulder, his pelvis hurt excruciatingly. Several times a day, a fluid washed through his body dispelling the pain and sending him off into strange dreams. He crossed lands that were unmoored from Earth. He became the moment when the dawn wind rises. He wandered in places entirely unfamiliar to him. The pain receded. But nothing relieved his sorrow and all that a soul experiences from a deep wound.

In this wan world, cool as a cellar, life seemed imperfect. A shadow was missing from the many at his bedside. The world without this shadow meant nothing.

All sorts of smells floated through the air. One scent was missing. Without that scent in the air, the atmosphere was unbreathable. He latched onto the idea that the tube in his mouth was keeping him from smelling the missing scent. With much effort, he managed to eject the tube from his throat. Suddenly there was activity all around him. Hands pressed powerfully on his lungs. Lips attached to his mouth. A panicky breeze stirred around his bed. There was a great deal of commotion, which he didn't like. He felt guilt for causing so much anguish and fevered effort. The commotion lasted a long while. Then everything fell back into an enormous, a secretive calm.

#

That night a woman appeared to him, seated on the edge of his bed, her eyes marveling at him in the eerie whiteness that filled the cubicle. Fingers brushed his face, a kiss grazed his cheek. Sweetness, consolation radiated through the room. He relaxed into the peace of the moment, savored the outpouring of tenderness. He had recognized the woman at his bedside. His mother's presence, vision of truth, spark of life, acceptance of trespasses, miracle of affection. At last, he had reconnected with his previous life. Yes, nothing truly disastrous happened on Route 17.

The day brought back its freight of noise, of comings and goings, of suffering.

Everything seemed flat and pointless, a long boring wait. He hoped the miracle would re- occur, that the beloved person would again bring light to his night hours. He watched time pass, contemplated the succession of nurses, listened to the desolate voices of men, these strangers in white who had made him a thing, their thing, who saw him as a piece of flesh, who punctured his skin without precaution, who appeared and disappeared, who cast an arrogant glance at him, sovereign beings, fathers superior, believing they were the essential condition for his survival, speaking amongst themselves as though he didn't exist, ignoring the presence that eclipsed them all, ignoring that a single voice now ruled over night's ghosts.

And once night had fallen, after his preparations for turning in, after his father's departure, after the last visit of the final white coat, she reappeared.

It became their new rendezvous, each evening, at dusk, when men's sadness is at its peak, the beloved face would materialize in the pale glow of the lamp that the night nurse always left burning. He would find his mother sitting at his bedside although he had heard not the slightest sound of footsteps or creaking of door or window. It didn't surprise him, just as nothing around him surprised him. She always sat in the same place, at the head of his bed, wore the same radiant smile, and started her visit with a song, always the same, "Love Me Tender." Her voice sang true, the melody was sweet. Afterward, she would look at him for a long while. He allowed himself to be observed, let her call him "my little angel." She would rise, take a compress from a table near the bed, sponge his forehead, wipe his lips, carefully examine the temperature recorded that day, the pulse rate, the blood pressure, the medications taken. The slightest good news sent her into transports of joy. A 98.6 and she was jubilant. A 120 over 80 and she gave him a hug. But she could also show anger if his fever climbed or his pulse rate accelerated. She would rage at the doctors, call them incompetent, vow to speak to the director. She knew the director. Most of the time, though, she seemed happy enough. His limbs had recovered their movement. His wounds had started to close. Things were improving.

One night she decided it was time for him to stretch his legs. He followed her outside. He wasn't at all surprised to walk there, in the semi-darkness, along a lane bordered with ancient oaks. He didn't feel the cold. He wasn't afraid of getting lost. He walked beside his mother in the tranquil night. Had he already seen that facet of the world? He didn't ask himself. He had eyes only for her. He took satisfaction in the moment. He lived a whole lifetime in that one moment. The time for revelations was past. Nothing could now change the course of his life. He didn't know whether they'd reach the enchanted shores. He was afraid not. Joy would not gush from the arid earth. He'd had his share. He was resigned to his portion of endless suffering, just as he'd subscribed before to boundless happiness. They had lived the best part. What more could they ask of the universe? Sometimes he would run. She loved to watch him run. He would race off as fast as possible, fly ahead, then run in circles around her. She would take a few strides too. Nights running beside his mother. They would return to his room, she would cover him with kisses, wipe the sweat from his brow, oh, he was his mother's angel. A white glow would suffuse the room, signal the start of day. Suddenly he would be alone. The wounds on his shoulder, head, and back would revive. And the wound in his soul burned like an inferno.

Waiting for dusk to come, he projected himself in thought to the windowsill, his secret joy increasing as the hour advanced. He would prepare himself for the coming reunion, impatient to see his adored mother, quietly allowing the women to clean him, urging them in his mind to scrub his skin hard, do your best, ladies, wipe away every bit of blood, the white coats always leave traces of their needle sticks, rid me of the dross that might startle a mother's eyes, every mother feels pain at the sight of her son in the condition doctors leave him in, do you think Mom any different from other mothers? Leave nothing that might frighten her, nothing that might look neglectful or suggest that Scott is not following Mom's advice, a mother's word is law, you know this, you are mothers too, trim my nails neatly, make my teeth gleam, the teeth are important, and shake a few more drops of that cheap perfume on my neck, it is the scent she will carry back with her into the darkness, rub hard, dear ladies, you are cleaning up an angel, Meredith Hatford's angel, and you, white coats, when will you remove these tubes? Do you think a boy receives his mother like this, on his back and bristling with tubes, almost naked and wasted to skin and bones, do you think this place befits a son? Put away these wheezing machines, do you want to scare Mom away, do you think you have every right because you have all the power? You know nothing, you're not even aware of the woman who comes to visit her son at nightfall.

At the end of the last night, his mother bent over him. A spectral pallor veiled her opalescent beauty. She looked distraught. Her palm grew colder to the touch, her expression darkened. In his dream, he saw his mother say goodbye. And for the first time he opened his eyes.

His eyelids parted. Dawn light was all around. He noticed the curtains at the window, the white walls, the railings around the bed, the room's emptiness. He abruptly understood what the men knew, the fate assigned to him, the form of challenge he would face. He realized the misfortune that had just befallen him, a misfortune without end, greater than wells watered with a million tears, hymns carried on the wind, the songs of a clamoring army, suns flooding into valleys, the smell of Earth's trees, the discovery of new worlds, the sidereal archipelagos, the golden harvests of the past. His mother had returned to the kingdom of the dead. He'd left her alone in the uncertainties of night. He'd slept warmly in his big white bed, while she walked in the absolute cold. He understood the prayers that men address to God, the Eternal, the infinite to which we give a name. His suffering was more than infinite, his despair would last beyond eternity.

A nurse came into his room, gave a startled cry. There was a rush to his bedside. An entire tribe of white coats gathered around him, with a strange smile on their lips, a conniving smile, joyful expressions radiating from their faces, their cheerful countenances conveying relief, satisfaction in their work, a limitless confidence in scientific progress, a deep faith in the forward impetus that governs the course of the world, banishes doubt, suspicion, and suffering. There was jubilation as though a holiday had been announced because his eyelids had parted. The simple movement of his ocular orbs brought cheers. Not one of the scientists seemed to see the beloved corpse stretched at his feet. Are you unaware, sirs, of the tragedy befalling me? Good doctors, eminent men, are you blind and deaf? Put away your joy, dress in solemn garb, this room is a graveyard. This decisive progress that you're making much of is a foot in the grave! You there, who were on duty, you with the smile on your face, did you not see a shadow glide into the night? The doctors exulted, congratulated each other, celebrated their day of victory fittingly. Champagne corks popped at Mom's funeral.

At dusk, he found himself thinking his mother would reappear. What use was sight if he no longer saw her face? Let them sew his ey elids shut, let him find grace again! He scanned the tops of the centuries-old oaks lining the alley as mist slowly enclosed them. The night passed and nothing happened. At dawn, he realized that day would come without his having seen his mother. Autumn would draw to a close. Winter and spring would elapse without her. Summer would be a synonym for nameless suffering. He was embarking on his life with no mother.

XIV

That morning, a procession of white coats entered his room, led by a tall, big-bellied, gray-haired man the others called "Professor." They surrounded his bed making a hubbub that the professor silenced by snapping his fingers. A young doctor stepped forward and in a solemn, slightly hesitant voice summed up Scott's history as he understood it: this adolescent, the victim of a serious car accident, after two weeks in coma, had recovered the use of his senses and his motor faculties but not his power of speech. The professor then took the floor, asking himself in a slightly ironic mode what could be the nature of the problem, before querying his students about what he called, in facetious tones, an "enigma of science." The doctors came forward one by one to inspect Scott under the professor's sardonic gaze. They auscultated his heart and lungs, palpated his stomach, examined his throat, peered into his ears, opened his eyelids wide, shined a bright light on his pupils, tested his reflexes, ordered him to stick out his tongue, tense his mouth into a smile, raise one hand, clench his fist. His reactions were carefully recorded. A machine was wheeled next to his bed, and small metal needles linked by cable to the machine were driven into his scalp. A sheet of paper started to unscroll. The marks were analyzed with care, sorts of conclusions were drawn. A physician remarked on the striking improvement in the patient's condition. Something continued to mystify them. There was nothing to explain his loss of speech.

One doctor raised the possibility of myocardial stunning. Another hypothesized a cerebral lesion. A third argued for the benefits of electroshock therapy. He discussed its advantages, its efficacity, its lack of harmful side effects. Electroshock seemed the panacea. A doctor who had been silent until then spoke the word "lobotomy." A new current of interest stirred the air. A poll was taken around the room. Those opposed carried it, and one of the doctors left the room to the accompaniment of sputtering laughter and quiet mockery. The professor stepped in. Where, pray, did they think they were? The room was silent. The man continued to speak in a loud, firm voice that inspired fear and respect, approaching Scott's bed and looking deep into the boy's eyes with an accusatory stare. Who was this young man to block the progress of science? The professor straightened and opined laconically that the time had come for reflection. The full extent of the problem had still to be grasped. The case wasn't simple. The doctors filed out of the room with hushed voices.

Late in the morning, his father arrived. Scott closed his eyes the moment he saw him. The man kissed his cheek gently, adjusted the pillow, pulled the sheets back into place, undid the top button of his pyjamas. Scott cracked his eyelids the tiniest bit. His father was wiping the top of the bedside table, refilling the water glass. He took the washcloth hanging near the bed, sponged his son's face, moistened his lips. He placed his palm briefly on his son's forehead. His face grew worried. He called to a passing nurse in the hallway, said he was worried that his son might have a fever. The nurse examined the chart at the foot of the bed. His temperature had been fine only an hour before. Jeffrey Hatfield expressed concern. His son's forehead was very hot. The fever could have risen in the meantime. The nurse agreed to take Scott's temperature again. The thermometer read 101 degrees. The nurse poured aspirin into a glass and made Scott drink it. His father begged her to call a doctor's attention to the fever. She promised to mention it when the doctors made their rounds. Wouldn't it be better to let them know right away?

He sat on the edge of the bed, slid his hand into his son's, tucked him in carefully, stayed a long while at his bedside, motionless, silent.

It didn't make sense. The grief-stricken man by his bed was all that was left of his former life, the living reminder of his torments, the stubborn evidence of past scenes. He'd always beaten Scott, always despised him. Now he was caring for him, showering him with affection. He was trying to be the quintessential father.

Scott opened his eyes again once his father had gone. He didn't want his affection, he wouldn't take his extended hand. His father's tenderness was objectionable, his kindness rang false. How could he believe in the man's sincerity? He'd lied from morning till night, lied to himself and others, used every variety of falsehood to his advantage, lied purposely and by mistake, lied to cover up his errors and his misdeeds, denied the evidence looking into another's eyes, lied knowingly and unknowingly, lied about basic things and anecdotal nothings, lied for the pleasure of it and to safeguard his pleasure, lied to those who loved him and to those who hated him. His life had been nothing more than a gigantic hoax. The man felt no guilt about anything, came to his son's bedside as though no tragedy had occurred on the road to Denver. As though life could continue after what happened on that road. The man had no sense of transgression. He didn't care about doing good. He didn't recognize evil where it lurked. The word "remorse" had no meaning for him. He buried even the memory of his wrongs. He was the king of impostors.

Scott remembered the time when, three or four years ago, Mom had caught his father red- handed in a lie. She set aside her grief, managed her anger. She wanted to understand. She had faith in the word of God and the word of men. Rather than make accusations, she found excuses for him. When his father came home, she gave him a lecture: lying is a fool's game. Lies take you in the wrong direction. They drag the liar down, undercut the person lied to. They make consciousness fragile. They debase and drive mad. His father didn't interrupt—at that point he was still capable of listening. When she stopped speaking, he said: "Are you finished?" She nodded. "Can I get up?" She said yes. He left the house. She felt a sense of euphoria, convinced that her words would go on resonating in her husband's mind. She said, "You'll see, Scott, it will take time, but it will have been worth it, right?" It made up for all her suffering.

#

The hospital staff continued to behave as they always had, acting as though he weren't there, speaking in front of him as if he couldn't understand—since he was dumb, he must be deaf—chattering about everyday things while performing routine actions. A glove rubbed against his skin, a hand took his pulse, his veins were punctured. The voices cared little about his suffering as long as his temperature was normal, his pulse rate and blood pressure stable, his eyes open. "He looks good this morning," said one of the women polishing his torso with a horsehair wash-glove. "Look, he's got some color, the doctors are optimistic, they say he'll get back his ability to walk and all the rest, maybe not all the rest, there's one thing he won't get back, what a shame it is, too, such a good-looking boy and so clean-cut, but considering everything, I'd rather have my boy lose his eyesight than his mother, and I'm only thinking of his own good. Gladys Chapman tells me that she knew Meredith Hatford well, how awful to talk about a young woman in the past like that, the woman was a saint, that's fate for you, spend your life saving people in the emergency room but the day when you need help, no one! You've seen her husband, oh sure, he looks choked up about it, but he should have done his crying before it happened, some day I'd like to tell him, because Gladys Chapman says that Mrs. Hatford used to come in here with dark rings under her eyes night after night, it's fine for him to be crying now, men and their false pride, but these aren't things you repeat, you never want to interfere with other people's grief, never want to get too close to misfortune, you don't know what tomorrow will bring, what disaster lies in store for us, we all take turns, no point pretending to be above it, the sun never shines for long on the same people, even in our corner of the world where the sun is always shining, but whenever I feel happy, I make a point of hiding it, not because I'm superstitious, I'm just cautious, in case providence should ever take a close look at my lot and decide I don't deserve what I've got, though I don't ask for much, and maybe that's why fate has left me alone, I'm careful not to dream big dreams, I keep to my place, I wash the patients' backsides, you have the most glorious job in the world, Senator Delsey once said to me a long time ago, he'd been brought here in a coma, and the morning he recovered consciousness he looked at me wide-eyed, smiled, and said: the most glorious job in the world. But Mr. President, all I'm doing is washing you, I said, I called him Mr. President because these people like to be addressed that way, and they're always president of something, or, if they're not, they will be some day, and I noticed that saying Mr. President made me feel better too, it re- establishes order where there is none, reassures you about the world, because no matter what they say, the world needs order, and it needs morality too, doesn't it, Mr. Hatford, and the senator said: Oh no, Mrs. Milway, because he'd caught my name, those people have a knack for remembering names, real phonebooks, you aren't just washing butts, he used that word, what you are doing, Mrs. Milway, is purifying souls, that's what he said, souls, no one had ever spoken to me like that, and although I know a thing or two about being a nurse, I never imagined that I was handling souls, I've paid a bit more attention since, but once they're out of intensive care, people forget because they can wash their own backsides, so they look down on you, think less of you, they make a separation of powers between their souls and what's below the waist, and their soul is not within your reach anymore, I wonder if they don't regret having talked to us that way, confided in us, allowed us deep into their private selves, Senator Delsey never even said goodbye to me, although he gave Dr. Murphy a gold watch, as if the big doc didn't have enough gold watches, whereas even a gold-plated one would have made my Christmas, but I don't mind, he can stick his watch where the sun don't shine, I never look at the time anyway, which is maybe why Fate and I keep at arm's length, I've seen too many of them pass through here, people scheduled down to the last minute who get swept up by eternity. Right, I think we're done with this good-looking boy, he's as soft and clean as the day he popped out of his mother's belly, may she rest in peace, I'll just take his temperature and then it's on to the next room."

Pastor Simpson paid him a visit. Scott didn't acknowledge the hand that squeezed his. He ignored the pastor's presence. He pretended that God did not exist. He heard the pastor's words: "A great misfortune, Scott, has befallen us. Every passing is a tragedy, but the tragedy here is compounded by a terrible scandal. How can we restore warmth to your wounded heart? Normally, a man of God has the answer to everything, a solution for the small ills, and an explanation for the great misfortunes. We hold the keys. We hold the encyclopedia on living your life and the dictionary on the hereafter. The Lord dictates words to us, I can attest to it on the Bible. But I have to confess, son, I spent the whole day searching and found nothing. I listened hard and heard nothing. Of course, I could say the usual things, the ways of the Lord are inscrutable, the Lord giveth and the Lord taketh away, all praises be upon Him. Speak the usual words and pray with you for the safety of her soul, but what's the point of praying, we shouldn't be imploring heaven for Meredith Hatford's salvation since Meredith Hatford's place is not in the heavens, your mother's place is here among men, to your left, on Sundays, in the fourth row at church, and at the emergency room services in Memorial Hospital on weekdays. I know I shouldn't be talking this way. My words are no help to you. I should reassure you that her death was not an accident, that in swerving off the road she followed the Lord's path, that this collision was an act desired by God, part of a plan too vast for mortal understanding.

I should find a meaning in all of this, a logic called Divine Will, disguised as the truck that crushed your mother. I should tell you that your mother is a saint, that the place for saints is at God's side. It would be another lie. Your mother is not a saint, she's a woman unlike any other, her place is among other women. I'm talking like an unbeliever, I'll no doubt be damned. I have tried to find the truth, but truth is nowhere, I have seen the heart of men and it is pure and without stain. Woe to him that is alone, when he falleth, says Ecclesiastes, but are we not all irremediably alone? For, as it also says in Ecclesiastes, we are to fear God alone, but what I fear, Scott, is that more misfortune will befall you. Before I came into this room, I told my soul, Quiet your heart, raise your spirits, unlearn your pain, I said to my soul, bow before the work of the Lord, for only wisdom is sweet, and only humility can soothe. But my anger is too great for me to quiet my heart, I'll come back tomorrow, or the day after."

#

At the close of the day, his father returned. He placed his hand on his son's forehead, smiled in satisfaction, examined the chart at the foot of the bed. Then he pulled back the sheets, uncovered his son's legs. He started to massage his calves and thighs, speaking as he did so:

"Calves are important, in the army we used to say you should always rub them. It keeps the veins from clogging, apparently. And the thigh muscles, they're important for a born runner like you, we don't want them to atrophy. You're going to be darting around here soon. I know the nurses also massage you, but a father can do it just as well, if not better. Muscles are our department . . . You're going to get well, son, it's just a rough patch that you're going through, I've seen men recover from worse wounds, you're strong, sturdy, your wounds will close over, your legs will heal, we'll walk together, even if I limp, I'll go with you wherever you want, I'll walk behind you if you're still ashamed of my gimpy leg, but you won't be ashamed, I know you, son, you don't hold grudges, you don't hate, and one day you're going to talk. The doctors don't know anything, they think you've lost the power of speech. You'll talk when you feel like it. We'll have conversations, if you want, even if I can never find the right words, but the sentences will fall into place as long as you're listening. I'm practicing, you know. There's something I say over and over again, night and day. I say I'm sorry."

Those through whom misfortune arrives, those who live in the light of grace, those to whom we owe our existence, those whom we consign to be struck by lightning, those who elicit out regret, those toward whom we pray, those who have always spoken truth, those who lie on every occasion, those who've found peace, those who've found death, those we cry for, those who shed tears, those drawn to despair, those who keep hatred alive, those who surrender to fear, those who surrender to misfortune, those who heap abuse on others, those who live on the sweetness at the heart of things, those for whom everything comes to an end, those for whom nothing ever starts, those who have waking dreams, those whom the sunrise consoles, those to whom dusk brings despair, those who believe in a series of random events, those who believe that all is foretold, those who live in the moment, those who insult the future, those who live in scraps of the past, those who plunge into darkness, those who walk toward the light, those on whom their parents dote, those who would kill their father and mother, are they all equal before God and man?

XV

That morning, Dr. Jenkins turned up at his bedside. Scott had heard the nurses say that the man visited him every day, ever since he'd been hospitalized. But his behavior raised eyebrows. The nurses described Dr. Jenkins as looking sad when he entered the room, devastated, although he was normally lively and jovial, they said the mood persisted unreasonably. His attitude wasn't in keeping with his position. He needed to get a grip.

Scott wanted to find out more and pretended to be asleep. Dr. Jenkins glanced at the chart at the foot of the bed, took his pulse, applied his stethoscope to Scott's chest, listened to the heartbeats, smiled, hung the device around his neck, grabbed the chair beside the bed, placed it in a corner of the room next to the window, and sat down. He stayed motionless, his eyes staring, deep in his own thoughts, as though sunk in prayer.

Scott would have liked to ask the doctor questions. The man had worked with his mother for years. He knew a lot about Mom. He knew tons of things that Scott had no clue about. He knew Meredith Hatford when she was not at her son's side. Was she still as sweet? Did she radiate as much joy and delicacy? Was she a different woman?

Scott parted his eyelids. Dr. Jenkins smiled. The boy would have liked to speak. Even at this moment, no words came from his mouth. The doctor stroked his hair, said he would come back tomorrow, and left the room. Would Scott some day know the woman who had been his mother?

An image came into his mind. He remembered when, a year earlier, he had accompanied Mom to Memorial Hospital on the pretext of writing a paper about nursing. She'd warned him: "You won't be able to stand it even for an hour." He'd stayed the whole afternoon. She'd soon forgotten that he was there. He wrote down notes in a big notebook. He felt he'd entered another world—the one that was all too familiar today. The smell of chloroform pervaded the emergency room, the sound of low voices, and every movement seemed charged with tension, every statement loaded with obscure meaning. The patient's groans, the staff's remarks, everything was sober, solemn. No gesture was innocent. Something critical, whose meaning he could not quite grasp, was playing out at every moment. The unit swarmed with patients. Ambulance workers wheeled stretchers in. People arrived on foot, limping, or supported by a friendly shoulder. The cubicles filled up and emptied out. People clustered in the hallways. A line formed outside, then broke up. No matter how fast Nurse Hatford and Nurse Chapman worked, the waiting room refused to empty. The whole town seemed to suffer from a complaint. His mother would leave one cubicle and go straight to another. Scott followed her with his eyes. She would pass by without noticing him. It wasn't really his mother. She'd lost her usual gentleness. Her glance was almost steely. At times, she moved like an automaton. She would wade into a crowd of men and women. She went from one patient to another, seemed to repeat the same actions, say similar words, her voice almost a monotone. She appeared to feel no fatigue, she absorbed grief, she absorbed pain. Suffering streamed over her. All the faces looked the same. She gave brisk directions to one family to wait outside. She didn't mince her words when someone was uncooperative. She pulled the curtains shut, he'd lose sight of her. When she reappeared, people would press around her, ask for preferential treatment. As the hours passed, her face grew paler. She started avoiding people's eyes. She walked between the rows of beds indifferently. The fluorescent lights blurred all faces. Hands reached out to her, eyes tried to catch hers. People in pain grabbed her by the arm. Sometimes her nurse's uniform and cap made her look like an angel. Sometimes she looked like a soldier at the front. Nothing seemed to stem the flood of patients. Adolescents would appear, moaning or laughing. Old people, lying on gurneys, gasped faintly.

Men would flinch with pain when she touched their stomachs. Others hardly remembered why they were there. More came, their breathing strained, their foreheads sweaty, they showed with a flat hand the place on their chest that was ripping at their heart. Others spoke in exalted tones that echoed through the hallways, announcing the end of the world, the coming of the Messiah in the wake of the Apocalypse. They looked to Mom for a sign of approval, and when they detected her doubt, they would erupt into insanity. They called her crazy, threatened her with the wrath of the gods, insisted on seeing someone else, someone sensible, someone who believed in divine justice, lived in fear of the Lord, respected the laws and commandments, preferably a man. Scott prepared to intervene. He would teach them a lesson. But Dr. Jenkins appeared and managed to cool tempers. As the hours passed, the endless suffering of the town paraded by. Mom didn't turn away from gaping wounds, didn't flinch at the sight of blood. In the middle of the afternoon, a wave of listlessness overcame her, slowed her movements, clouded her voice. She barely responded to questions, reacted sluggishly to calls for help. She went out to get a little air and smoke a cigarette in the back room. When she returned to the unit, her voice was firmer. She looked straight at people again. She attended to whispered confidences, spoke words of comfort. The faces in the ward registered gratitude.

Around 7 p.m., the emergency room finally emptied. Around her, all was calm. Time to go home. They'd taken the bus. She'd slept during the whole long trip back, her face drawn, her features tensed, her lips trembling ever so slightly, as though the world's suffering, kept at arm's length all day, had come to trouble her dreams.

#

That time was over and done with. Never again his mother dozing beside him, the sound of her soft breathing, the moments of grace watching over her all the way home, I am my mother's guardian. It was his turn now to spend his days with Dr. Jenkins, walk along the edge of the abyss, pass through the door where eternity starts, hear the word "hello" as if it were a farewell, speak to the ghosts of night, endure suffering without knowing hope. He had landed in the part of the world where light-heartedness was a thing of the past. The shadow place where his mother was no longer living.

#

Mike entered, greeted his cousin, looked at the skyline out the window, sat down. A nurse came by to ask what he was doing there, listened to his explanation, and left. "Wow, did you see that girl? Some people have all the luck! Those legs! I don't care what you say, those uniforms are the cutest. OK, not something you can fully appreciate in your condition . . . Holy Toledo! Did they ever get you but good! Look at that! Your nose, the shape of your nose, say, does it hurt when I press here? Anyway, girls don't care the kind of nose you have. Even in Hollywood they couldn't care less. Look at the one Robert Mitchum's got and then look at Kirk

Douglas's, one's a potato, the other's a knife blade. Can I look? I heard they put a screw in your shoulder, and you've got broken ribs and broken bones in your back, you're a real battle casualty! You know, what has them all puzzled is that you aren't speaking, they don't know that you're the quiet type . . . Hey, I have to tell you what happened while you were out, even if it didn't come to all that much in the end. There wasn't a war, you probably figured that out. President Kennedy won, he made Krushchev back down, JFK is a born actor, he lies like an actor, dresses like a prince, and on top of that he sleeps with actresses! So let's see. . . my adventures with Alison don't really interest you, but I can tell you that I'm not too far from the Holy Grail, I'll get there in a week, two at the most. What else . . . Oh, I have to offer you my condolences, and I'd rather do it now because it's never a good time. I also want to tell you something: I've always known that your mother didn't like me, but I liked her a lot. I've never met anyone kinder or sweeter. So if she didn't like me, I'm sure it's because she was looking out for you . . . We're kind of alike now, you and me, since I don't have a mother either, even if it's different, mine died so young that I never really missed her, I don't have any happy memories to hold onto, maybe in a sense it's better to lose your mother early on, it saves you from being sad about it . . . Anyway, I'm all the family you've got now, along with your dad, so yeah, you're going to come up a little short on kind-heartedness, it's not exactly a big trait in the Hatford family. All the same, things have gotten better since you left. I've seen your dad cry, more than once, so there's something of a silver lining to it. Oh, and the main thing is that you've moved, your father has rented an apartment in Phoenix, we're all going to live there together, form a real family, although he's starting a little late, I know. OK! I promised the nurse I wouldn't stay too long. They say you're in pain, even if it doesn't show on the outside, and apart from your nose and the screws in your arm and the fact that you can't speak, you're good as new."

#

That night, his father came back to see him. He closed the window that had been cracked open, pulled the curtains shut, glanced at the chart, turned off the ceiling light, lit the bedside lamp, adjusted the sheets, filled the water glass, picked up a piece of paper lying on the floor. He sat next to the bed, put his hand on Scott's, and started talking in an uncertain voice.

"Dr. Murphy wants to call in a psychiatrist to find out why you aren't talking yet. I said no. You're not crazy, son. There aren't any crazies in the Hatford family. There's desperation, yes, but no insanity . . . I know you'll talk one day. We'll talk to each other. I'll tell you things I've never said to anyone. You don't have to be scared of me anymore. I'll never raise my voice to you again. I'll never raise my hand to you . . . Show forgiveness, son. You know, everyone is not made the same. Some are flawed. We have big cracks running through us, life seems impossible to handle. We buckle under the weight of some unknown defect. We beg for a respite, even a small one. We'd do anything to enjoy life's offerings without getting that bitter aftertaste in our mouths. We try our best. We swim upstream against life's current. We struggle through imaginary floods of fury. We walk in a thick fog. We don't see the sunny side of things. Black clouds of unhappiness line our forward path and our back trail. We draw unhappiness to us, and spread unhappiness around us. We've lost all forms of courage and instead feel hatred for every living thing. We're blind to the riches of the world. Our faces in the mirror horrify us. Our own voices frighten us. Our least memories turn our blood to ice. Say you'll forgive me, I know the extent of my own guilt. I've lied every time I opened my mouth. I've insulted the memory of the dead, I've defied the Lord, walked in pride, despised my fellow man, hated humankind, caused terror. Forgive me for turning every dance into a funeral. I've threatened my immediate family with death, and death has come. I idolized violence, abused my strength, I struck with my fists, struck with my belt, I gave in to fits of insanity, I wallowed in drunkenness, I've humiliated, I've cheated, I've put my arm around every whore in Rolder. I've committed every crime, Scott, but I'm not a killer."

Through the slit between his closed eyelids, Scott watched his father. He looked at the man's eyes. Those eyes had seen his mother for years, night and day, month after month. Had some part of her been imparted to him, in spite of himself, over the course of time? A dollop of kindness, a fragment of tender feeling might have transferred to him? Was it possible that the years left no residue, no mark, were gone entirely? He looked deep into his father's eyes, tried to catch a special glimmer there, some reflection of Mom's face, an imprint time might have left, inscribed for all eternity. He thought he saw a glint.

#

Long after his father had left and while Scott was drifting off to sleep, he felt a hand brush against his hair. He opened his eyes and saw Jenny's face as she leaned over him, her big gentle eyes, her mischievous expression, her red lips smiling broadly, her blond hair cascading in curls down to her shoulders. Her long slender fingers ran lightly over his cheeks and lips. She said: "Hey, little Elvis, you aren't in the best shape, look at the dent on your forehead, look at your nose, what have they done to my lover-boy's face, but luckily Jenny's here to pamper you, because what you need is tenderness, and, as it happens, I'm good at tenderness, they say that I'm all gentleness, that there's delicacy in my whole body, poor little angel, your father told me, he was passing in front of the coffee shop, I ran out to him because I was so upset that you were gone, I'd never seen him with that expression on his face, usually your father looks as though he has it in for everyone on earth, but here it looked like the weight of the world had fallen on him, when I asked him what was wrong, he looked at me with those blank eyes I'd never seen before, since his eyes are normally spitting anger, but now he was no longer the same man, the legendary hothead that, deep down, I liked OK, he wasn't out to get anyone, not that he seemed reconciled with his fellow man, more that he was no longer one of them, as if your dad had set himself to the side and was now watching others pass, you must have noticed that too, you're the kind of guy who notices things, but hey I'm not here to talk about your father, even if he's the one who told me your news, and also your mother's, the two of you go together, I only met your mother once, but I've said the effect she had on me, so I can imagine how it is for you, since you saw her on a daily basis, but if I you don't mind my saying, and in spite of how much grief you feel, you also have cause to be joyful, you've known happiness every day, that's a gift from heaven, even if, obviously, providence snatched it from you too soon, the gold you had in your hands, providence gave you a taste of happiness and then, whammo, a mouthful of misfortune, but can you be angry at providence, no, you can only thank heaven, OK, so I say that but, you can't find your consolation in the past, so I've come to bring you a little comfort, not that it's much, but I'll give you what I can all the same, since your sorrow affects me, but you'll see, I'm a bit of a magician, sorrow goes elsewhere for a time when you're with me, and that's worth a lot, here, give me your hand." She took his hand by the wrist. "I know you don't want to talk, so open your eyes wide." She unbuttoned her shirt, her hand still grasping his. She was next to him with her breasts uncovered. It was unlike anything he'd ever seen. She took his hand and put it on one of her breasts. "Feel how soft it is?" It was soft and squashy, succulent and smooth, and exquisitely tender. He'd never felt such a thing at the ends of his ten fingers. "You haven't seen anything yet." She climbed up to kneel on the mattress, straddled his pelvis, raised her skirt, sat on him. Then she pulled the sheets down, lowered his pyjama bottoms, grabbed his penis, slipped her panties aside, quickly slid his penis into her, arched her back, moved back and forth along his penis, insisted that he look her in the eyes. But he couldn't keep his eyes open. He felt himself sucked toward an unknown place, every sensation was like lightning, made him dizzy and light-headed, brought him to the edge of a blackout. He closed his eyes for fear of falling into the chasm that his body was dragging him toward. She grabbed his other hand, placed it on her other breast. "Look at me or I'm leaving." He did and was astonished. She'd taken off her shirt and her extended torso filled all of space, her breasts, two perfect spheres, flaunted the laws of gravity, floated, their large pink nipples staring at him like round eyes, her skin and the pallor of her soft unclothed body seeming to give off light. He couldn't take his eyes off this body shaken by jerky breathing, this endless body that still seemed too slight to hold such a quantity of beauty. Her captive splendor rippled wonderfully, her carnal authority dispelled every other image, driving back the shadows, the ghosts, capturing all of the ambient air in its choppy breathing. And now the foretold miracle occurred, suddenly, a fraction of a second, at the moment that something detached itself from him, he was freed of his memories, released from his pain. She became motionless soon after, abruptly, her face as if twisted in pain, then suddenly calm. Then she withdrew, sat on the bed, grabbed his penis which now lay soft in her hand, slipped it under his pyjama bottom, which she raised into place, rearranged the sheets, buttoned her shirt, kissed him on the forehead, and left the room. He immediately fell into a deep sleep.

That night, he had a dream. He saw Lieutenant Hatford, wearing a helmet, carrying a rifle, a pack strapped to his back. Lieutenant Hatford stands tall, in a barge cutting through the waves toward Normandy's beaches. Around him are the men in his unit, their features drawn, fear in their bellies, hanging on their leader's words. The lieutenant's face remains expressionless. His heart acknowledges no fear. His eyes look straight ahead at what would terrify the most valiant of men. Squatting in their places, his troops try to suppress their terror, they pray, their eyes lifted toward heaven, haunted by the fear of losing an arm or a life. Jeffrey Hatford doesn't allow his feelings to show. The nothingness that lies ahead doesn't frighten him. Blood will flow, rivers of blood. Terrible premonitions bombard him as the launch approaches the coast. He is gripped by a strange madness. He insults fate and taunts death. Along with strength, a secret tenderness emanates from him. His soldiers see it as unflinching resolve, disgust for gratuitous brutality, horror of the arbitrary. The sound of the machine guns swells, terror rises in all hearts. Nothing is visible beyond the line of helmets. The metal platform is the horizon line that meets their eyes. No one knows what's coming. No one claims to have a fate.

The future starts and stops at this moment and in this place. From his men's souls, a boundless love arises, at the same time as an enormous anger rumbles. Suddenly the barge opens. Waves and breaking surf appear, a stretch of sand beyond it, a swarm of men moving toward the beach, a wall of cliffs rising in the distance. The soldiers wait for Lieutenant Hatford's orders. His words hold the fate of the men around him. He bellows the order they've been waiting for. They make the big leap. The water slows their bodies, fear paralyzes them, their heavy packs keep them from moving, their orders are lost in the chaos. The sea, the sky, the earth fill with horror. Bullets whistle past. Helmets float on the water. Lieutenant Hatford plants a foot on the sand. He stays at the water's edge, waiting for his men to pass him. He counts heads, who comes out of the water, who stays in. He yells orders that no one hears, makes gestures that find no audience. His eyes see nothing specific. His mind suggests nothing concrete. The bullets cut down his men. He starts to run. Are his feet tripping over men's stomachs or heaps of sand? He continues to shout orders, mechanically, in vain, the order to advance, the order to fire, the order to hit the dirt, the order to get up, the order to run. His shouts are lost in the din. What is going on around him looks like nothing he has ever imagined, nothing anyone has told him, nothing known. He has never before seen a man die, and here, this morning, all the men are dying. And the bodies of the living look like those of the dead. There is no place he can turn his eyes to shield them. A single thought obsesses Lieutenant Hatford: leading the living to the foot of the cliff.

XVI

He couldn't get used to his new surroundings. He hated the white walls. Looking out the window, he couldn't see the desert, he couldn't see Route 17. His mother's scent never drifted through the room. The photograph of Mom that his father had put on the little dresser didn't answer when he spoke to her. His room was the center of a world that had disappeared. The sun rose, they opened the curtains. Night fell, they put out the lights. His father, his cousin, the entire staff of Memorial Hospital showed great solicitude toward him. Nothing made any difference. The universe held no promise. Life had lost the source of its luster. No adventure was worth undertaking. Why go to the moon now that his mother wouldn't be waiting for him on his return?

The round of visits, the comfort offered him, the shows of support held no interest for him. Once night had fallen, he walked alone across the high plateaux, climbed the crests of mountains, hurtled down into the depths of valleys, everywhere there was the same pale, trembling light, the same emptiness, in all the universe nothing resonated other than the echo of his memory and the noise of his suffering.

His father, who visited him morning and night, would ask him what he wanted, if there was anything special he'd like to eat or drink, if he felt better or worse than the day before. He bought novels and read from them, a few pages at a time, in the evening. He read poorly, speaking unclearly, he stumbled, stuttered, tripped over words, he put no expression into it, no emotion in his voice. None of the characters came to life, none of the stories held together. But he kept at it. Before leaving Scott's room, he would say a prayer. His prayers sounded false. He'd never prayed in his life. He didn't know anything about the Lord. His prayers would never ascend to heaven.

Scott was given permission to get out of bed. At first, it was just to take a few steps around his room, hanging on his father's arm. Then they started walking outside, along the wide alley lined with ancient oaks that he saw from his room. He bared his eyes to the burning sun. He looked at the blue sky, glimpsed in the distance the tops of several tall buildings. When his father took his arm away, Scott felt for a moment as he had when his mother was teaching him to ride a bike and he'd suddenly found his balance. Then his legs buckled.

His father would talk to him when they were alone, alert for the slightest trace of a response, the tiniest sound. Scott never uttered a word. His father said: You've walked again, and you'll talk again. The doctors were apparently resigned. His father wouldn't give up. You'll leave the hospital when you're fully recovered. There's no reason for you not to get well. His father had always denied the obvious. He failed to see the why of things.

#

Scott decided to run away. He needed his mother just the way he needed oxygen. He wanted to revisit the place where Mom's presence still hovered, even if his father no longer lived there, even if the house was deserted. One morning, he dressed, slipped out of his room, left the hospital, took a bus to the main station, climbed aboard the Greyhound shuttle, got off at the stop in the middle of the valley, crossed the outskirts of town, entered Rolder, walked along Lincoln Ave, crossed Roosevelt, Capitol, and Hawthorne streets, reached Seneca Square, then climbed Blank Street to his house. He paused a few seconds on the porch, hesitated before pushing the door open, overcame his fear. Once through the door, he felt swallowed up by the house's stillness. He closed the door behind him. Everything smelled of dust. A pale light filled the silence. A broken chair sprawled in the middle of the kitchen. Nothing of what he knew was left. The bare walls were unrecognizable. He felt like an intruder in his own house. He entered his room. In a corner, on the ground, he saw a piece of the president's photo. He followed the hallway to his parents' room. He hesitated before opening. He remembered the day when, just as he was about to go in, he'd heard muffled sounds of breathing and low voices. He put his ear to the door but heard nothing. He decided not to go in. The sound of footsteps on the porch made him jump. The door opened. A great flood of light washed into the room. His father's outline filled the doorway, his body large and hunched over. A gust of wind swirled through the house. His father walked toward him. Three feet away, his father stopped, his eyes locked on his son's, his face sad, sorry, gentle. His father took a step toward him, his arms wide open. A nameless fear took hold of Scott, an irrepressible feeling that became tinged almost immediately with shame. He'd have liked to fly into his father's embrace, feel his strong arms around him, inhale the desperation in his breath, forgive the man who had confessed his faults, exonerate a soul that was complicit in the greatest of crimes, this accidental killing, share misery and consolation, drink with him from the cup of grief and suffering, join him in strewing the grave with imperishable flowers, sound the truce, forget revenge, and heal the wounds. But he took a step to one side, slipped around his father, broke into a run, flew out the door, crossed the garden, and tore down the path.

When he had almost reached Los Lobos, he turned to look back. His father hadn't followed him, or he'd been outdistanced. He ran better than anyone. His legs had come back to him. Almost everything would come back, a nurse had predicted at his bedside. The town of Rolder sprawled at his feet, sunk under a covering of mist, laced with veiled pleasures, a sanctuary of life, a theater of great tragedies. Beyond it lay the desert with, running down its middle, the gaping fissure of the accursed road where his childhood had ended, the route of misfortune, the path of angels. On this road in the distance, a bus was moving, which he recognized immediately as the Greyhound bus from Phoenix. He followed the vehicle's progress, the cloud of gray smoke rising behind it. His heart started to beat. He felt the blood pound at his temples. He started to run. He raced down the hill, flew past the Mexicans' house, ignoring the teenager who, as Scott passed, drew his thumb menacingly across his throat. He arrived at the bottom of Blank Street and entered Rolder's street grid. He followed Hawthorne, then Roosevelt, got a boost of energy when he saw Mr. Brown raise his head from under the hood of his car and shout out, "Go get 'em, Scott, this time you'll make it!" He angled off between the warehouses, feeling wings on his back. He was Willie Williams and Bob Hayes, he was all of the Dodgers, half cheetah and half man. He had the impression of splitting the air in two. Every step gave him an extra bump of speed, each stride was longer than the last, he stretched time, jostled the seconds, his feet hardly touched the ground, he felt uncatchable, invisible, invulnerable, the fastest boy in the world. He could reach the bus stop before the shuttle arrived. Today would be a first.

He shot past the last house in Rolder and burst into the valley. Now he was flying along Route 17, running higher and higher, faster and faster, the muscles in his legs and thighs possessed of superhuman force. His head rose into the clouds, he outran time, left a horde of ghosts trailing in his wake, heard the distant voice of a woman urging him on. He glided through space. He passed Owen Each's ranch, saw Ted on his stallion, who encouraged him with a twirl of his lasso. For a moment, he felt that he could run faster than a horse at full gallop. Suddenly he saw the bus racing toward him with its headlights on. About a mile away, he could see the bus stop rising out of the flat, naked land, the center of the desert and the center of the new world. The sight re-energized him. He sped up. He no longer felt subject to the laws of gravity, the laws of nature, the laws of God or man. The heavens would soon proclaim his victory, in this magical world beyond time and space. The wind at his back pushed him, while the bus in the distance grew closer, the sound of its motor growling in Scott's ears. He would get there before the bus, despite the tea kettle sound in his lungs, the loud pounding of his heart. Man would triumph over machine and win the race against time. He ran, wild with happiness and joy, he was returning to his realm, he was advancing toward the past. And he, alone in all the world, knew toward whom he was drawing near, whose hand he would soon be taking. He didn't even dare think her name, for fear of provoking God's anger. But he harbored a mad, a deep-seated conviction, and the breath of wind at his back supported his belief, whispered that he was right, and the only condition for the miracle to occur was that he accelerate even more, reverse the course of time, invert the time of tears and the time of joy. He would wrest from fate a portion of his own destiny. Will alone was capable of great feats in

the vast grandeur of America. The powerful voice of the pioneers
and the breath of God sang the resurrection of a radiant beauty. A
burning bush had appeared in the desert, why would the Heavenly
Father not make further miracles? What had he believed in
throughout his childhood? What did Pastor Simpson teach them?
Parting the billows of the Red Sea, walking on water, a last
miracle was still to be accomplished. Hadn't he prayed, and with
fervor, all those Sundays? How could he not be rewarded? He ran
in the bright sunlight, the angels hovered around him. O Lord of
hosts, I have never doubted, and if I doubted it was only for the
briefest moment. Make all the curses I have uttered null and void,
the oaths of rebellion, You are the Almighty, You will see to it that
my hopes are not in vain, Your mercy will plead in my favor, You
will reestablish justice, You will grant my prayer, You will atone
for Your transgression, for You have transgressed, Lord, You will
repair Your crime, You will find the strength to accomplish this
miracle, Almighty God who supports the weak and heals the sick,
Your breath imparts movement to the dust. From motes of dust,
You will forge a rib, and from this rib You will fashion the body of
a mother, Your breath will pass into her lungs, and her body will
live again, you will make her appear here below, at the very
moment the door opens, the door of heaven and the door of the
bus, don't fail me, Lord. You will fulfill your promise of
resuscitating the dead if I fulfill mine, if I accomplish a miracle of
my own by arriving before the machine, winning my race against
time. Glory unto you, Immortal Lord.

He tagged the post that marked the bus stop, raised his head and saw the mountain ahead of him instead of the grille of the bus that normally confronted him. He was out of breath, drenched in sweat, horribly thirsty, but flooded with a feeling of absolute happiness. He had done it. It was a first. This was the hour and the day. He'd won his race against time. Man had triumphed over machine. The feat had been accomplished. His fate now lay in God's hands. "I believe in you, Lord, who has promised to resuscitate the dead." The sound of brakes startled him. His heart pounded. His temples were about to explode. He was on the verge of experiencing grace, he would sing the Lord's praises forevermore. He wouldn't reveal the miracle to anyone. He would never speak of the resurrection. They would leave the area together, his mother and he. No one, ever, would hear of them again. Their names, the recollection of what they'd done, all trace of their presence would be erased from men's memories. The bus stopped in front of him. Thou art great, Lord, I believe in Thee. He waited for the door to open, the door to the bus and the door to heaven. His mother would appear from behind that door. Had not misery lasted long enough? He had won a victory over time. He had done what he needed to do. He made the sign of the cross, raised his eyes heavenward. The door opened. The conductor waved to him: "Hey, Scott! Glad to see you back, and looking stronger than ever! Coming aboard?" He shook his head. "OK, see you soon." The door shut. The bus took off. A cloud of gray smoke forced him to close his eyes. When he parted his eyelids again, a wasteland lay in front of him. Not a soul anywhere, not a breath of life. The air lit conflagrations in the plain. No object cast a shadow, everything scorched the eyes. He felt a wave of extreme fatigue, as a deep sorrow welled up in him. He sat down. The earth around him was desiccate and bare. The sky clouded over. Everything exhaled sadness. He had tried all a person might. He had challenged death, had wanted to resuscitate the first light. He had been the plaything of a strange madness.

Who would walk down the valley beside him? He had lost the living symbol of his dreams, the inspiration of his days, the constant object of his attentions, his source of joy, his consoling spirit, the sacred object of his affection, the foundations of his universe, the grace pervading the world. Now night had won.

The sound of an engine drew his attention. He saw a car in the distance driving toward him. The car slowed. He stared at the man behind the wheel. He was tempted to run away. His legs refused to carry him. The car stopped when it came abreast. He exchanged a glance with his father through the window glass. The door on the passenger side opened. His father's face wore a look of deep quietude. How could he stay so calm when terror and suffering had engulfed the world? His father cut the motor, took a lighter from his pocket, lit a cigarette. He looked at his father, uncertain what to think, what to do. Should he go sit next to his dad? Those he sat next to met with disaster. Who was to say whether, without him, his father would have gone over so deeply into fright and anger? Lord, is everything that happens my fault?

"Would you like to come to Phoenix with me?" his father asked gently. "I'm pretty sure you'll like the apartment that Mike and I picked out. Your room is enormous, you know. I'd like you to come with me. I'm not going anywhere without you."

Scott looked down at the ground. Sobs surged in his throat. He managed to hold back his tears. He nodded yes, slid onto the seat next to his father. The car sped off down the road. He looked at the new horizon distantly taking shape in the daylight ahead of him.

XVII

The seconds ticked by, the hours elapsed, the days filed past. His grief stayed with him. The months alternated, summer bleached the grasses, leaves fell from the trees, the seasons changed. His grief stayed with him.

His room filled with furniture, the walls acquired posters, the bookshelves filled. His rancor gave way. Resentment no longer governed his actions. Hatred for his father no longer ruled his thoughts. His anger, which had turned inward on himself, he could sometimes suppress. His sadness never.

The president had been assassinated. The people he cared for were passing away.

His memory for facts was no longer very specific. He couldn't attach a date to certain events. On what day had Mom read the letter addressed to the mayor? Was it on October 22? When did she talk to him about Elizabeth Taylor? Now he could only say: On Sundays, we would go to church. Every morning at 6 o'clock sharp, I would set off to meet my mother. Time was swallowing up the past.

He thought: "I've lost my mother, I've lost my voice, I could lose my memory." Mom could disappear from his mind as suddenly as she had left this world. He constantly poked and prodded his memories. He loved the way the old days had been. He shied away from any moments that would divert him from thinking solely about his mother. He dreaded the dancing reflection of the stars, the song of birds at sunrise, his cousin's cascading laugh. He hated the first light of dawn that he had so loved before. He expected nothing, and nowhere did happiness or his mother await him.

#

Only my suffering remains. The sharp radiance of day, the shadow of the mountains, the whims of time, the sorrow of dusk, the mystery of forests, the tranquility of deserts, the blind anger of men, the fulfillment of desires, words of condolence, comforting talk, advice given—all change over the course of time, all seem to undergo a cycle like the seasons'. I've understood, Lord, where you live. You reside entirely in grief and suffering. You reside in misery and pain. I know now where your greatness is centered.

You are wholly hidden in my unhappiness, my boundless agony and my never-ending woe. You alone are infinite, You alone are eternal. You inspire my suffering and You nourish my pain. You are the other name of eternal grief. You will help me watch over my mother until the end of time.

I've learned to recollect myself with a simple look toward the sky: I dig a grave in the middle of the clouds. I lift up my eyes and walk in the cemetery where my mother rests. I walk there during the day, I walk there at night. I proceed among the stars, I walk on the moon. Mom, I didn't lie to you. I've never lied. I keep my promise every day. I am the first man to walk on the moon.

XVIII

The car stops in the middle of a stretch of sand dotted with prickly pear bushes. He casts a glazed look at the misty landscape. His father opens the passenger door for him. A scent of amber and musk wafts over him. The trees rustle in the wind, and from beyond them comes the murmur of the sea and its powerful echo.

"Here we are, son!"

His father pulls a bottle of orange juice and a plastic cup from a bag, fills the cup, and hands it to him. He drinks it to the last mouthful. His father offers him cookies, chocolate chip cookies from Flare's Bakery. He gobbles them down. "Some fruit?" He is fine, no more, thanks. "Maybe later?" Maybe. He gets out of the car and stands looking at his father.

"Is my outfit making you laugh?"

His father is dressed as a cowboy. The hat is too big for him, the trousers are sliding down his hips, the shirt is printed with green checks, around his neck is a clumsily knotted red bandanna. He is holding a lasso and looks thrilled.

"Aren't you proud of your father?"

#

They'd set out from their apartment in Phoenix the night before. His father drove all night. Nothing in his face hints at fatigue. His eyes sparkle with intense joy, as though this man who fought in two wars and conquered an entire continent expects on this day and in this overlooked place to take part in an adventure beyond anything the modern world has known.

The mist rises to reveal clumps of eucalyptus and willow in the distance, their leaves fluttering in the wind. Beyond them, the hillside drops away into the void. This is the valley of the East River, the place of myth, the site of ancient dreams.

His father opens the trunk of the car and starts unloading the carefully packed gear, two lightweight, frameless saddles and a second lasso. Owen Each explained to them that the mustangs wouldn't stand for a western saddle, but that they would accept a very light one.

He watches his father unpack everything. Is the man serious? Does he really believe that mustangs will emerge from the mountain's recesses? And if the miracle happens, does he think he'll be able to ride a wild horse with his bad leg?

"I worked on a ranch in the early 1950s. I even rode the rodeo circuit!"

His father is telling tall tales. The world around him is a fable, composed of evil spells, strange enchantments, and sacred savagery, where hope-filled innocents set out for barbarous lands, their hearts at peace, and become lost on dark trails. A fable whose moral he is vainly seeking. The man with a limp, the dumb boy, the princess with the naked heart.

#

"All right, let's go!" They walk down the trail, each carrying a coiled lariat over his shoulder and gripping a light saddle. "Let me go first, it's full of snakes." They cross the scrubland.

"See, son, thanks to my gimpy leg, we're sure to find our way home." His father's left shoe traces a long straight groove across the ground, making Scott smile.

"I'm making you laugh this morning, aren't I? But we're not going to be laughing in a little while. We're going to save a mustang from drowning."

His father's gone mad.

At the edge of the grove of willows, the man asks for a stop, badly out of breath. He takes off his hat, mops the sweat from his face, sprinkles his head with water. "You're thinking I'm too old for this, aren't you?" They set off again, his father still in front. They walk to the edge of a plateau, push through a small forest of pines.

"Look!" says his father.

Scott walks to where he is standing and sees a spectacular landscape, incredibly magnificent and calm, the sea extending to infinity, the sea he has never seen except in dreams, or else at the movies, but it's different here, sublime, grand, an entire world before his gaze, sparkling brightly under the vault of heaven. He feels dizzy at the cliff edge, looks down and sees below him the country Mike has talked about, the crescent of sandy beach that the horses are said to cross before sinking into the waves. The hill on the other side drops gently down to the calm and peaceful spot where the waters of the East River form a broad pool. "Are you ready?" He nods. He braces himself for disappointment.

They start down the hillside along a rocky trail lined with trees. An eagle with a monarch's profile circles above them, everything is exactly the way Mike described it. A few yards ahead, his father drags his foot over the stones, almost tripping at every step. From time to time he says, "Are you hanging in there, son?" Scott makes a point of letting him lead by several yards. A mark of respect.

The boy looks at the landscape flooded in light, the big pines adhering to the rock faces, the cliffs dropping down to the water, hollowed by caves. He thinks he can hear the clamor of Indian tribes, White Belly's war cry mixing with the muttering of the waves.

They have descended to the foot of the hill and halt on a flat rock by the river, watch the East's currents swirl tranquilly past them, the surface of the water ruffling in the breeze. "This would be a good time for a dip. Do you remember when I taught you to swim in the arroyo in Rolder?"

Suddenly, a muffled rumbling sounds from the depths of the gorge, echoes off the faces of the surrounding hills. He thinks of a storm. He looks at the sky, the sky is cloudless. A truck rattling along the road? No vehicle could cross a ravine like this. He scans the horizon looking for an airplane. Is he hearing things, the way he used to hear voices in his room?

"Look!" says his father.

…An apparition. A group of horses trots in Indian file along the opposite bank. A bay stallion leads the little troop. Behind, two old roans move peacefully. A pinto mare is followed closely by her colt. He rubs his eyes. "No, this isn't a dream!" The horses pursue their way, their coats shining in the light, their nostrils opened wide, their eyes sparkling in the sun's glare. Mike wasn't lying.

The beasts enter the river, water splashing around them. The sound of their hooves, the regular laboring of their lungs fill the air. The sight is astonishing, more beautiful even than in his cousin's telling.

Scott suddenly remembers the fate that awaits these animals.

"Don't worry, the first three mustangs are old, their time has probably come. But we won't let the mare and her colt drown themselves in the sea." From his long practice of interpreting Scott's silences, his father can read his thoughts.

The cavalcade comes abreast of them.

"My turn, now!" His father twirls his lasso. The rope whistles through the air, adding its own note to the animals' concert. The horses sense an alien presence, stop. Scott observes the mare's eyes, sees no trace of fear in them. The colt circles around his mother. The bay stallion shakes his head, whinnies, stamps his feet and starts off again at the same slow pace, followed by the other horses. "I'll get the mare. The colt will stick by her, and you can ride him." The man twirls his lasso again and throws it toward the mare. The loop falls over the animal. The slip knot slides down her neck. The man jerks the rope, the loop tightens. The mare stands stock still. His father gives a powerful tug. The rope stretches. "You hold the rope, now!" His father tosses him the free end. Scott clenches his hands around it as tightly as he can. The mare looks toward him. There is no hostility in her eyes, no distress. Scott is moved, thinking that her eyes have looked over unbounded space, over the russet plains in autumn, the misty winter sun, the fury of nighttime storms. His father walks toward the mare with a sure step. The leg trailing behind seems not to hamper him. The horse jerks backward, gives a long whinny. The other horses stop, turn their heads, then set off again at a trot. His father presses against the mare's shoulder, whispers in her ear, and pats her back. The mare backs away, pulls harder against the rope. His father strokes her nose, keeps talking. The colt rubs his muzzle against his mother's rump. The mare shudders, raises her ears. His father shoots his son a glance, gives him a determined look, makes the signal. Scott tugs sharply at the rope. Lord, may I be equal to the occasion, may I keep the mare and her colt from escaping out to sea!

His father drops the light saddle onto the mare's back. He strokes her neck. The animal accepts the saddle. His father grips the mane tightly, throws his leg over. When he is firmly seated on the mare's back, Scott releases the rope. He slowly approaches the colt, careful to make no gesture that might spook him. When he reaches him, he remembers the advice Ted Each gave him when he was learning to ride. He pats the animal, talks to him in his mind. The colt offers no resistance. Scott passes the loop of his lasso over the colt's neck and settles the saddle in place. He lifts himself onto the colt's back, pressing against his shoulders. Then he squeezes his flanks and feels himself carried by the colt's movement as he walks beside his mother, his mane floating in the morning breeze.

They ride slowly, his father and he, along the river to the sea, then along the beach. They urge the mare and her colt onto the sandy soil. They reach a place where the hill rises gently. They lead the horses along a path between boulders and tumbled rocks. They trot for a spell, then stop by a stream where they water the horses. "I think we did it, son! We'll find a ranch somewhere around here that will take these horses."

Scott absorbs the sound of the stream, the soughing of the wind, the smell rising from the warm earth, the panting of the animals, the burning memory of what he has just lived through. He experiences enormous joy. The sun is now high in the sky. Usually there is a long, menacing shadow between him and his father. This morning, the sun is shrinking the shadows.

"Scott, do you think our faults can be forgiven?"

Scott casts his eyes over the mare. He looks down at her feet. Something is wrong. He examines the colt's feet. Both horses are shod. The mare and her colt are not mustangs. No more than the bay stallion and the two old roans, probably. Now he understands the horses' strange calm, their apparent docility, the fact that the mare never snorted, never reared once. He realizes what happened. His father stage-managed the cavalcade using tame horses from Owen Reach's ranch. Mike, who didn't join them on the pretext of a migraine headache, drove the animals down to the East River. The horses were wild only for the time of his waking dream.

His father made his dream a reality. His father pulled off a magic trick. His father is a sorcerer. The Houdini of the Far West.

He looks at the mare and her colt, relieved to think that a mother never leads her young towards its death. He starts to laugh.

"Is my question so amusing?" asks his father, with a sudden expression of sadness on his face.

He shakes his head. He feels guilty for the pain his laughter is causing. He raises his eyes toward the sky. He thinks he sees his mother's figure among the clouds, her gentle aspect. She walks in the enchanted panorama of the world, each gesture inspired by grace, her bright eyes shining with the heavens' azure glow, she ambles, an angel among angels, her face radiant, wearing the same cheerful expression, impervious to terror, that she made a point of showing him before she passed away, an eternal face, vibrantly sweet. He can clearly hear Mom's voice murmuring something, but her words are mixed with the noisy breathing of the horses, the burbling of the stream; his mother's encouraging voice, an unquenchable song dropping from the firmament that seems to talk to him and no one else, the only witness to her final hour. Her soft slender hands, dipped in the celestial air, leave eddies in the wind, reviving her scent, the smell of her hair, the odor of her skin, dispersing the horrible cries of that frozen night where his past overwinters and his memory grieves. Perhaps some fine day, the pure radiance of the sky will light his days?

"Joking aside, Scott, do you believe our faults can be forgiven?"

He nods his head yes, with an emphasis that leaves no room for doubt. He takes his father's hand, squeezes it, turns toward him. Jeffrey Hatford looks at him with gentle eyes. He thinks of the man in uniform who, years ago, before misfortune hit him, won his mother's heart with a single glance during a bus ride. He tells himself that maybe it is the same man. Then he plunges again into the great silence of the day.

By Laurent SEKSIK

Novel
THE LAST DAYS
Pushkin Press

Graphic Novels
MODIGLIANI
with Fabrice Le Hénanff
Salammbo Press

THE LAST DAYS OF STEFAN SWEIG
with Guillaume Sorel
Salammbo Press

Play
MODIGLIANI
Salammbo Press